Tangled in Time

Tangled in Time

Lynne Fairbridge

RONSDALE PRESS

RONSDALE PRESS LTD.
3350 West 21st Avenue
Vancouver, B.C., Canada
V6S 1G7

Set in Minion: 12 pt on 16
Typesetting: Julie Cochrane
Printing: Hignell Printing, Winnipeg, Manitoba
Cover Art and Design: Ewa Pluciennik

Ronsdale Press wishes to thank the Canada Council for the Arts, the Government of Canada through the Book Publishing Industry Development Program (BPIDP), and the Province of British Columbia through the British Columbia Arts Council for their support of its publishing program.

CANADIAN CATALOGUING IN PUBLICATION DATA
Fairbridge, Lynne.
Tangled in time

ISBN 0-921870-69-8

I. Title.
PS8561.A5472T3 1999 jC813'.54 C99-910600-7
PZ7.F1607Ta 1999

to my beloved husband Pete,
my dearest mother Pam,
and to my good friend Hazel who
has given so much of herself
this past year.

ACKNOWLEDGEMENTS

I would like to thank Ronsdale Press for their patience and support. Many thanks also to Mom, Natalie and Kevern for retyping the manuscript when the original electronic version vaporised at a crucial point; to Mrs. Elsie Navis, an editor of *A Furrow Laid Bare,* who vetted the Neerlandia portion of the manuscript for agricultural and historical accuracy; to Mae Koene for her assistance with Dutch; to Merle Harris for her advice regarding historical resources; to Gwen Molnar for checking the accuracy of the historical details of early Edmonton from her personal experience; to Brenda Bellingham, Inge Israel and Monica Hughes for reading and commenting on the manuscript, and to my family and friends whose support made it possible to complete the book. Finally, my thanks go to the Alberta Foundation for the Arts for the grant which made it possible for me to undertake this project.

Chapter One

The scent of lavender filled Janna's nostrils as Omie opened the door. "This will be your room," Omie said. The room was tiny, crammed with a high carved bed, a heavy mahogany dressing table, and a chest of drawers covered in bric-a-brac. "I put up new wallpaper and I hung that painting you liked when you were a little girl." Omie pointed at the pale pink rosebud covered wall.

Janna's eyes turned eagerly to the painting above the bed. The last time she had seen it was before Opie's heart attack. It had hung on the wall of their living room in California, and to Janna there had been something magical about the cool dark pool half hidden in trees. But there was nothing magical about it now. It seemed sombre, rather dull. Janna was disappointed but not really surprised. Everything changed.

"What a cozy room," Janna's mother, Vivian, commented, peering over Janna's shoulder.

Omie nodded. "Isn't it? It used to be much larger, of

course, before the house was divided — part of what used to be a study."

Footsteps clattered down the passage and Janna's little brother thrust his curly blond head into the room. "Do I sleep here?" He dived towards the knick-knacks on the dresser. "Look at that tiny little dog! Can I have it?" His fingers closed on the ornament.

"Come with me, little love," Omie grabbed his hand and prised the dog free. "Let's give Janna time to unpack and I will show you where you're sleeping. You and your mother are sharing a bedroom upstairs."

"Will you be all right in here?" Vivian asked as Omie steered Roddy out the door. "You can sleep upstairs with Roddy if you prefer and I'll have this room."

"She'll be fine," Omie called. "Come along Vivian. Janna's a teenager now and needs her privacy."

Grateful to be alone after the long, cramped car ride, Janna dumped her suitcase on the floor, settled on the bed and gave an experimental bounce. The mattress was soft and springy and she threw herself back into the down quilt. Perhaps it wouldn't be so bad being here for a while. She hadn't wanted to miss two weeks of school to come to Edmonton, not because of school but because of Steven. They'd only just become friendly and she was afraid that if she stayed away too long he would forget her. Her mother said that if their relationship didn't survive a separation then it wasn't a real relationship, but that was easy for her mother to say. Still, she was glad to see Omie again. Even though

Janna had seen her grandparents only every two years or so, Janna had always adored Omie. Her mother said that she and Omie were very much alike, in looks as well as in personality.

Also, it was good in a way to get away from home. There were so many painful memories all through the house. This was the first holiday the family had taken since Janna's father had been killed in a car crash fifteen months ago. Dennis, a neighbour who had been a friend of her father's, had offered to drive them to Omie as he had to make a business trip and planned also to visit his parents in Edmonton. Vivian said the opportunity was too good to miss. Janna sat up and hugged her knees as she thought of Dennis. He had been very kind since her father had died. He had helped her mother sort out her father's belongings, and he had helped with the legal arrangements as well. He had spent a lot of time with the family. Just lately, Janna had begun to feel that it was too much time, although she found her feelings hard to explain, even to herself.

Shutting off her thoughts, Janna scrambled off the bed and pulled back the heavy plum velvet drapes. Outside, raspberry canes ran down the centre of a long backyard dividing it into two narrow rectangles bordered by a caragana hedge. In the centre of the lawn on Omie's side, Janna could see a large crabapple tree newly leafed in translucent spring green and on the neighbour's side, a silver haired old man on his knees in a vegetable patch.

As she turned away, Janna glanced at Omie's picture

again. It was bathed in a shaft of pale spring light from the window and it seemed to Janna there was a ruffling in the foliage at the foot of the trees, as though the leaves were touched by a breath of wind, or, as though someone hiding there had stirred. Janna caught her breath. It was exactly what she had sensed before, in California. Once, she even thought she had glimpsed a woman.

"Janna..." There was a tap at the door and her mother poked her head into the room.

"What?" Janna muttered, tearing her gaze reluctantly from the painting.

"Dennis called. He wants us to go and meet his parents. Try and find something decent to wear. I'd like to make a good impression."

"Now?"

"Dennis said he'd pick us up in half an hour or so."

"What do we have to meet Dennis' parents for? We've only just got here."

Vivian looked flustered. "Dennis just thought that we might like to. Apparently he's told them all about us and they're looking forward to meeting us."

"I don't want to come," Janna said. "I'll stay with Omie. You can leave Roddy if you like," she added, as Roddy barrelled into the room behind her mother.

"Omie said you have a magic painting," he squealed excitedly. "I want to see it."

Janna scooped him into her arms. "I'll show you."

"It's not magic," Vivian objected. "You know it's just your imagination, Janna. Don't you go filling Roddy's head with all kinds of nonsense."

"Look," Janna said, holding Roddy up to the painting. "See those bushes? If you watch carefully, you might see a lady hiding behind there."

"Where?" Roddy glanced briefly at the painting and then wriggled free of Janna's arms. "I want to hold the dog," he said, hurling himself towards the china poodle.

"You'd better come with me." Vivian caught him in mid-flight. "And perhaps you're right," she went on to Janna. "I'll suggest to Dennis that we wait until another day. How about he takes us all for a drive instead and shows us a bit of Edmonton? We could take Omie and stop for ice cream and pizza. What do you think?"

"I want ice cream!" Roddy said, clambering onto the bed beside Janna. "Can I have ice cream?"

"Why don't you go without me and..."

"You have to come, Janna!" Roddy protested.

Janna kissed the top of his curly blond head. Although what she really wanted to do was to have time alone to examine the picture, Roddy looked so like her father that it was hard to refuse him anything. "All right," she said, casting a rueful glance at the painting.

Dennis picked them up half an hour later and they drove into the city centre. It was a typical modern city: tall glittering bronze and copper glass buildings. Dennis parked the car and they walked across the high level bridge to admire the view. "The bridge is 157 feet high," Dennis said as they stared at the North Saskatchewan River shining like a ribbon far below. "When it was built in 1913 it was the fourth largest in Canada and very unusual because it had an upper deck for the railway and the streetcar and a lower deck for pedestrians and cars." Dennis was an engineer and liked bridges. He grinned at their blank faces. "But I suppose I'm boring you."

"No, no, Dennis, it's very interesting," Omie replied. She pointed across the river at a stately domed sandstone building. "And that's the Alberta Legislature and the one farther in the distance that looks like a palace is the Hotel Macdonald."

"Which was built by the Grand Trunk Pacific Railway in 1915," Dennis added.

"When are we having ice cream?" Roddy asked.

Dennis hoisted Roddy onto his shoulders. "I guess that's enough of the grand tour. Let's get to the main event."

It was evening when they got back to Omie's but Dennis accepted Omie's invitation to stay for soup and a sandwich. "I love the house," he said as they sat around Omie's kitchen table, after Roddy had been put to bed.

Omie nodded. "I grew up in Edmonton and I always loved this neighbourhood. You know, when I moved here after Opie died, Mitch, Vivian's brother, tried to talk me out of buying this house. Omie's folly, he calls it. He wanted to put me into one of those sensible retirement complexes, but I wouldn't have it. I'm very happy here and I have such a nice neighbour, Judy Mason. She's been very kind."

"I saw an old man next door," Janna said.

Omie lowered her voice. "That's Judy's father. She keeps suggesting I meet him. She made some joke about fixing me up with him."

"Maybe that's not such a bad idea," Vivian said with a smile.

Omie frowned. "Old men like him have only one thing on their minds — all they want is someone to cook and clean for them. You wouldn't believe how many propositions I've had since Opie died — old men popping out of the woodwork like worms, all looking for a housekeeper, but that's not what I plan to do with the rest of my life."

Dennis laughed. "I'm not surprised you're sought after. The soup's great."

"What we need now," Vivian said, "are those chocolates I bought. I think I must have left them in the car. Be a pet and get them Janna."

Janna jumped to her feet. She had been impatiently waiting to leave the table. She wanted to write the postcard she had bought for Steven while they were out, and she wanted to look at Omie's picture again. Of course, her mother was probably right and she was imagining whatever it was she thought she saw. But still, what if . . . ?

Outside, the evening air was heavy with the scent of the

lilac hedge, which lined the front yard. Janna paused, breathing in the heady perfume.

"Beautiful evening, isn't it?" a voice said.

Janna started and look round to see the old man she had noticed earlier sitting on the neighbour's side of the porch. Remembering that this was the man who had designs on her grandmother, Janna merely nodded.

The man stood up and extended his hand across the railing, which divided the porch. "I'm visiting my daughter," he said. "Everyone here calls me Gramps."

Janna took his hand and grinned despite herself: the old man had such bright blue eyes and a wide smile. "I'm also visiting," she said. "I'm Janna."

"That happens to be one of my favourite names," Gramps said. He ran his fingers through a shock of silver hair. "I'm only here for another couple of days, but I hope we'll see more of each other."

It took Janna a moment to find the car. Omie didn't have a garage and Dennis had had to park a little way down the street in front of the apartment block beside Omie's. She retrieved the chocolates and sped back to the kitchen. "I won't have any," she said as she planted them on the kitchen table. "I'm going to read in bed for a while before I go to sleep."

Vivian took her hand and kissed her cheek. "An early night is a good idea," she said. "We have a fun day planned for tomorrow."

"Sleep well, little love," Omie said.

"Yes, sleep well," Dennis echoed.

"Goodnight." Janna frowned as she left the room. She used to like Dennis. He had come sometimes when she and Dad had gone to model airplane shows. Dad was a pilot and loved airplanes. And if something went wrong while Dad was away, like the washing machine, or once the bath leaked right through the ceiling, then Dennis always came over to help. Still, he seemed to think now that he was part of the family, and he wasn't.

Alone in her room, Janna couldn't think of what to write to Steven. Perhaps she shouldn't write to him anyway. Perhaps he would think that she was too pushy. Janna lay on her bed chewing the end of her pen. Steven was the first boyfriend she had had. She wasn't even sure that he was a boyfriend, except that he had given her a little furry gorilla holding a banana. She wished it had been a white teddy bear, which, she felt, would have made his intentions much clearer, but her friend, Melanie, insisted that a gorilla meant the same thing.

Janna propped her pillow at the end of the bed and gazed at Omie's picture. Above her, she could hear the sounds of Omie going to bed. As she lay watching, half concentrating, she sensed again movement in the bushes and branches which trailed over the shining still surface of the water. Intently now, not daring to move, Janna stared. She could see the branches tremble, and she could hear the leaves rustle as though someone was pushing the foliage aside. Something pale became visible behind the leaves. As Janna struggled to make out what it was, the shape drew nearer, and then a woman stepped out. She was slight, dressed in a long rose-coloured garment. She lifted her head and looked at Janna. Involuntarily Janna sat up, gripped by compelling dark eyes. She didn't know what happened next. Everything went black and she felt herself falling. A cold wind roared through her ears and she cried out; the sound of her voice echoed through the darkness.

The plummeting ceased suddenly. Janna opened her eyes, feeling disoriented and dizzy, and found herself kneeling on the floor on an intricately patterned oriental rug.

"Hello," a voice said. "When did you get here?"

Startled, Janna focussed on a pair of brown dress shoes standing in front of her. Her gaze travelled up baggy grey flannel pants, past a white shirt and suspenders, to meet the bright blue eyes of a boy of around her own age. Behind him, on the wall, she could see Omie's painting.

Chapter Two

Janna's mouth dropped open. "Who are you and what are you doing in my...?" The words died as she noticed a row of glass fronted bookcases below the painting. Her gaze shifted to a massive walnut double-pedestal desk where her bed should have been. She scrambled to her feet. "Where am I and how did I get here?"

"You're in the library, of course," the boy said calmly. "I've no idea how you got here. You must have been jolly quiet though to have got past Grandma. You know I'm not supposed to bring friends into the house. Why don't we go to the ravine?"

Janna studied the boy. He had a wide smile, a mop of dark curly hair and bright blue eyes, the colour of a summer lake. "I'm dreaming," she muttered. "And you're a figment of my imagination."

"If anyone's a figment, you are," the boy protested. "I was just wishing I had someone to talk to because Norm and Jeff have gone to their cabin for the summer and Neil's parents have gone East, and then there you were."

"Charles!" a high pitched irritable voice cried out. "Where are you, Charles?"

Charles grimaced and ran his fingers through his hair. "Unfortunately, Grandma is not a figment."

"Charles!" the voice repeated, closer by.

The boy grabbed Janna's hand and pulled her down behind the desk. "Quick, hide!"

Janna crouched uncomfortably beside him. The faded floral cotton dress which had somehow replaced her pajamas dug into her armpits. "I'm confused," she muttered. "Very confused."

"Ssh!"

"Why are we hiding?"

"Because you're not supposed to be inside and I'm supposed to be practising scales."

Janna leaned her head against the wall and studied the wallpaper, rust-coloured and embossed with a gold paisley design. "Ugly," she whispered.

"She can't help it; she's old." Charles yanked Janna to her feet. "Come on, she's gone. Let's go before she comes back."

"Where?" Janna asked, too bewildered to argue.

"I told you: the ravine. Grandma would never look for me there. I wonder if my skull collection is still there. I used to keep it in a hollow tree." He peered round the door. "The coast's clear. Follow me." He dashed down a long dark hallway that smelled of floor polish, through a kitchen, past a large woman enveloped in steam bending over an old-fashioned washing machine on legs, and out the back door.

"Charles! Is that you?" the voice shrilled as Janna fled, tripping in shoes which were several sizes too big, across clipped green grass.

"Did your mother see us?" he asked as Janna clambered up beside him into the branches of a crabapple tree.

"My mother? What's she doing here?"

"Laundry... You must have seen her. Ssh..." He stopped talking as a thin woman with steel-grey rigidly waved hair appeared at the doorway of what looked very much like Omie's house. She glared around the back yard and then marched back inside. "Charles!" she warbled again.

"We made it," Charles said triumphantly. He began picking hard green berry-sized apples from the tree. "Watch out! Here comes your mother. If we make a run for it, we can get to the hedge."

Janna peered through the leaves at a large bony woman staggering across the lawn carrying a wicker hamper piled with wet laundry.

"That's not my mother," she said as the woman dropped the basket and began to hang sheets on the washing line, but Charles had already launched himself towards the caragana.

Janna paused. What a strange dream this was. The details were so clear. She could feel the ridges of the bark under her grasp, the tickle of an ant walking across her wrist, and she could hear the flap of sheets on the line, the buzzing of a bee.

"Hurry!" Charles called, his face emerging from the hedge.

There didn't seem to be any alternative to following him. Janna didn't fancy facing the grandmother or the large laundry woman. She swung down from the tree and galloped towards him as fast she could in her clumsy shoes.

"Janna," a voice called after her. "Waare kom je vandaan?"

Glancing over her shoulder, Janna saw the laundry woman striding after her waving her arms. "Janna! Kom terug!"

Janna didn't slow down. She blundered through the thorny hedge and emerged in the alley, scratched, bleeding, and out of breath.

"That was stupid," Charles said, indicating a gap in the hedge.

"This whole thing is stupid," Janna muttered, glancing through the gap to see whether the woman was following her. "What was that woman saying? I can't understand her."

"I've given up trying to understand adults," Charles said as he sauntered down the alley towards the street.

Janna brushed leaves off her dress and pulled spikes of caragana from her hair. Charles was admiring an old car parked in the alley. He climbed on the running board and ran his hand over the polished hood. "Isn't this swell? It's a brand new 1933 Chev."

"It does look new," Janna conceded, looking at the shiny red car. It had mudguards over the wheels and headlights which looked like bicycle lamps.

Charles aimed a crabapple at a cat stalking along the back fence of the neighbouring yard. "It's as new as you can get. You can't buy 1934 models yet."

It took Janna a moment to grasp the significance of what he had said. "So you're saying this is 1933?"

"And what are you saying?" Charles aimed another apple. "Darn! Missed again. That cat ate a nest full of robins last week."

Janna reminded herself that she was dreaming. Still, the dream was making her uneasy. "Who are you anyway?"

Charles grinned. "You are being peculiar today. Have you lost your memory or something?"

"Maybe I have," Janna snapped. "Just humour me. Tell me your name, your full name and everything about you."

"Charles Randolph," the boy answered as they emerged from the alley onto the street. "Son of Michael and the late Elizabeth Randolph. Born on July 3, 1920, resident of Edmonton, Alberta, etc. etc. Who did you think I was anyway? Groucho Marx?"

None of his information meant anything to Janna. She bent down to try and tighten the laces of her shoes which clattered loudly on the wooden sidewalk. "So if you were born in 1920, you're thirteen now?"

"Same as you," the boy replied.

"Eeuw! What's that smell?" Janna held her nose and straightened up.

Charles pointed at a steaming pile of horse manure in the street. "The milkman was just here."

"He did that?"

Charles grinned. "You know I meant his horse. Come on, the ravine's this way."

Janna trailed behind him wondering how much longer the dream was going to last. Usually in dreams as soon as she realized she was dreaming, she woke up, but this time she hadn't. And this didn't feel like a dream. Janna closed her eyes and pinched her arm hard. The pain was sharp, but when she opened her eyes, Charles was still ambling in front of her, kicking a stone along the sidewalk. "Bozo," she muttered to herself, rubbing her arm. "That wasn't such a good idea."

"That's Mr. Bozo to you," Charles said.

"What?"

"You know — it's a line from *Duck Soup* — the Marx brothers' movie," he went on as Janna stared at him blankly. "My favourite part is where Harpo stands in the lemonade."

Janna was getting more and more worried. Stay calm, she told herself. Think clearly and everything will be all right. She forced herself to think back. She had gone to bed early and had lain on her bed. She remembered looking at Omie's picture and seeing movement. Then she had seen someone in the picture, and the next thing she remembered was suddenly being in Charles' library staring at his feet. Everything in the room had changed except Omie's picture which was on the wall behind him.

Janna stopped as a thought struck her. Was it possible

that the picture . . . No, it wasn't possible. Was it?

"You are a slow-coach," Charles called back, waiting for her.

Janna was deep in thought. Perhaps she should go back to the picture just in case. It was the only thing she could think of doing.

"Come on," Charles said.

Janna shook her head. "I've just remembered I left something in the library. I have to go back." Without waiting for his response, she took off in the direction they had come from.

"Wait!" Charles called after her, but Janna only increased her speed.

Back at the house she peered through the hedge. She could see the woman Charles had called her mother through the open kitchen door. She would have to try the front door of the house and see if she could get in that way. Taking off her shoes, she clambered over the neighbour's fence and cautiously made her way through the yard to the front of the house. To her relief, she reached the street and Charles' porch without being seen. Cautiously, she tried the handle. It turned and the door creaked open. Janna held her breath as she stuck her head through the crack and blinked to focus in the dull light.

There was no one in the dark panelled hallway. She could hear the loud tick of a grandfather clock at the end of the passage beside the stairs, and the muffled sound of what must have been the washing machine, but no voices. She eased through the door and tiptoed down the passage hoping to find the library. The first room she passed contained a grand piano and something that looked like a cathedral-shaped radio. She scurried to the next door and then dived into the room as she heard the sound of voices. She skidded past a long claw-legged dining-room table and flattened herself behind a display cabinet of silver.

"Tomorrow I will iron," the foreign woman said in slow and accented English. "Is there anything else you wish me to do today?"

"No thank you, Marie," Charles' grandmother replied. "You may go now."

Footsteps receded down the passage and then there was silence. As Janna crept towards the door, a newspaper on the table caught her attention. "Hitler Defends Action Rooting Out 'Bolshevist Evils'," she read. The date on the newspaper was June 1, 1933. Janna shivered. Could she really be in 1933?

At the end of the passage Janna had to choose between two doors. Her first choice turned out to be a storage cupboard. As she tried the second, footsteps sounded on the stairs above her. She flung herself at the door and stumbled into the library. In front of her was Omie's painting.

"Charles!" a voice called out.

Janna stared desperately at the painting, unsure of what to do. "If you got me into this," she whispered urgently, "get me out!" Behind her she heard an icy voice. "What are you doing in here?" At the same time, she saw the leaves in the painting tremble and a light flicker behind the branches. A pale figure emerged, gliding out from the foliage. And then there was another voice: "Get up now, Janna. Get up!"

Chapter Three

"Get up, Janna!" Someone shook her arm. "You're sleeping too long!"

Janna opened her eyes to find Roddy's face inches from hers. She could feel his warm breath on her cheek. Disoriented, she stared around the room. The walls were covered in tiny pink rosebuds, the dresser in ornaments, and her pillow was scented with lavender — she was back in her bedroom at Omie's. Janna felt a surge of relief followed by an illogical moment of disappointment — Charles had been only a dream.

"She woke up!" Roddy called, slithering off her bed. "Mom, she's awake. We can go now."

"Where are we going?" Janna called after his departing figure.

Roddy scampered back to her and scrambled onto her bed. "The waterpark." He began to bounce. "The waterpark! The waterpark!" he chorused in time with each thump of his feet on the mattress.

"Stop that." Janna groaned.

He stopped bouncing and flung himself at Janna. "Omie says that there are huge waterslides and Dennis says…"

"He's here?" Janna asked.

"In the kitchen." Roddy snuggled into the blankets beside Janna and put his cold feet against her leg.

"Hey!"

Roddy giggled and began to crawl his toes up her calves.

Janna grabbed his pink plump feet and began to nibble his toes. Then she tossed him off the bed. "You'd better get out of here and let me get dressed before I eat you all up."

However, Janna didn't get dressed after Roddy had left. She scrunched her knees under her chin, huddled into her pillows and began thinking about her dream. It was surprising how vividly she could recall all the details. Usually all she remembered of dreams were fragments which hardly made sense.

"I brought you some tea, little love," Omie said, pushing open the door. She put a mug beside Janna's bed and pulled open the drapes. "Shall I help you make your bed?"

Janna abandoned her dream reluctantly. "I can manage, thanks." She gulped down her tea and then dug through her suitcase for jeans and a T-shirt. Her bathing suit was also somewhere in there. She fished it out with mixed feelings. Like her father, she loved swimming. He had taken her to the pool almost every week, but she hadn't been much since he had died — it brought back too many memories. Still, the sun was streaming through the window and she had never been to a waterpark.

She put her bathing suit on under her clothes and undid the clasp of the locket around her neck. It was one her mother had had as a child and had a picture of her father in it so she didn't want to risk losing it. She tossed it on the bed while she shovelled the clothing on the floor into one of the dresser drawers.

"Are you ready for breakfast?" her mother called from the kitchen.

"Coming." Janna remembered Omie's offer to make her bed and hastily straightened the bedcover over her tangled sheets. As she did so, she heard the clink of something dropping and remembered her locket.

"Janna!"

"Coming," she shouted again. She could see the locket under the bed against the wall. She tried to push the bed aside so she could reach it, but the dresser was in the way. She shoved harder, and the bed moved, ramming the headboard into the wall, gouging the wallpaper. Janna groaned as she closed her fingers around her locket. A strip of Omie's new paper had ripped to reveal navy paper underneath. She tried to smooth the rosebuds back into place, but the navy paper was also damaged. Perhaps if she tore off the wrinkled navy paper, it would be easier to glue the rosebuds back in place. Concentrating, Janna folded back the strip of pink paper and began to tear away the blue. What she found took her breath away. Underneath the blue paper was another layer of wallpaper: rust, embossed with a gold paisley design.

"Janna, we're all waiting for you," Vivian said from the door.

"What?" Janna sat up, still dazed.

"For breakfast." Her mother helped her to her feet and steered her towards the kitchen.

Janna's mind was reeling. How had she dreamed of the exact same wallpaper that had once covered these walls? But there was no time for reflection or to re-examine the painting. Roddy couldn't wait a moment longer so Janna gobbled her cereal and toast, and they piled into Dennis' car for the waterpark.

But all the time they were at the waterpark, as she hurtled down the splashing slides or floated over the swelling waves, her dream was at the back of her mind.

"You're not watching me, Janna," Roddy complained, tugging at her arm. "I was swimming and you didn't see. Look." He launched himself in a flurry of arms and legs, churning a fountain of water that splashed over Janna. "Did you see? Did you see me swim?" he demanded when he stopped, gasping for air.

"That was wonderful, Roddy." She grabbed him under his arms and swung him around so that his feet trailing in the water made a shower of spray.

"Do it again, Janna," he begged when she released him, but Janna shook her head. She had caught sight of Dennis standing waist deep carrying her mother in his arms. They were both laughing. The sight triggered a memory of her father carrying her mother across a river the last time they had gone camping. She could see her mother's expression, head thrown back, laughing, just as she was doing now with Dennis. Janna felt sick as she watched them.

Roddy fell asleep on the way home in the car. "That's what I feel like doing," Omie said, as Dennis carried him into the house. "I'm going to have an early night tonight."

"Not too early," Vivian said. "I was hoping we could celebrate."

Janna's stomach tightened. "Celebrate what?"

Vivian giggled and glanced over at Dennis, who had put Roddy on the couch. "Dennis and I have something to tell you."

"What's that, dear?" Omie asked.

"You've probably already guessed," Vivian said.

Janna's stomach tightened. "What is it?"

Vivian took Dennis' arm and looked up at him with a smile. "We've decided to get married."

"That's wonderful," Omie said, kissing Vivian's cheek and then standing on tip-toe to kiss Dennis. "I couldn't be happier for you. Congratulations to you both."

Janna just stared. "But you can't!" she burst out finally. "What about Dad?"

There was an awkward silence. Vivian looked at Dennis. Omie looked at Vivian. "Janna," Dennis said eventually, trying to put his arm around her shoulder, "your father isn't coming back. You know that. But although I can't take his place, I will try my best to make us a family."

Janna pulled free and ran from the room. “I don’t want you,” she cried as she slammed her own room door behind her.

“Janna, can I come in?” Omie opened the door as she spoke. “I’d like to talk to you.”

Janna wiped away her tears with the back of her hand and looked over her shoulder. “You’re already in,” she muttered.

Omie settled herself on the end of the bed, crossing her legs at the ankle. “Little love,” she said, “I know it isn’t easy, but you have to try and let go of the past or you’ll make your life miserable.”

“I’m not miserable,” she said, “but I will be if Dennis comes to live with us.”

“You’ve always liked Dennis,” Omie reminded her. “Besides, you have to think of your mother. She’s been lonely since your father died.”

“So have I,” Janna retorted.

“Of course you have, little love, but it’s different for your mother. You have your school friends, a boyfriend I hear, a whole life ahead of you. She doesn’t.” Omie paused and there were tears in her eyes. “I know what it feels like to lose a husband and to face the rest of your life alone. It’s very very lonely.”

“Janna . . .” It was Vivian at the door. “I’m sorry I sprang my news like that on you. Please don’t be upset. I’m sure you will understand when we talk about it some more.”

Janna glared at her. "I won't understand," she said. "I still love Dad."

"And so do I," Vivian said. "Look, I know this is hard for you, but do try and be reasonable. We won't rush the wedding — you can be my maid of honour, and perhaps we can move to Edmonton so that we will be near Omie and Uncle Mitch — we'll be a real family again. I know you'll like that."

Janna felt as though she had been stabbed. Not only was she going to be forced to have Dennis living with them, but now Vivian was talking of moving! She would have to leave all her friends, and Steven. "I'd hate it!" she yelled. "I won't be your maid of honour. I won't even come to your stupid wedding, and if you move to Edmonton, I'll stay with one of my friends!"

Vivian turned white and Omie stood up. "You know you don't mean any of that, little love. Come, Vivian. Janna needs some time to think. We'll talk about this again tomorrow after a good night's sleep." She leaned over and kissed the top of Janna's head and then took Vivian's arm.

"I meant every word," Janna shouted after them as they left the room.

Janna crossed to the window and stood staring out. Anger and hurt throbbed painfully in her chest as long shadows crept across the deserted backyard. She could hear the sound of a piano coming from next door and the hum of distant traffic. A cat meowed and the old man, Gramps, let it in. The piano started again. Gradually Janna's anger subsided and loneliness, pale, grey, aching loneliness, took its place. Omie was wrong to think she didn't know what loneliness meant. She was often lonely. No one understood how she felt, particularly about her father. No one even talked much about him anymore. Roddy was too young to remember him well, and now, if Vivian forgot him too, he would become a ghost. But Janna was determined that she would keep him alive.

She dumped her clothes in a heap on the floor and climbed into her pajamas and bed. Perhaps sleep would provide a respite from the turmoil churning inside her. She closed her eyes. The sheets, filled with the soothing scent of lavender, felt smooth and clean against her skin.

A breeze ruffling the curtain and the moon shining through the window woke her some time later. Janna's eyes followed a pale path of light across the bric-a-brac on the dresser, over the shadows of the carpet, up the wallpaper, until they reached Omie's painting. It was bathed in moonlight, and beside the silver lake, a figure stood waiting. She looked up and met Janna's eyes. "Come," Janna heard in the stirring of the air. "Come."

Chapter Four

The figure stepped out of the painting, her face hidden by a sweep of hair, her long rose gown trailing behind her. She reached out pale fingers; her touch was a cold breath on Janna's hand. As the bed gave way beneath her, an icy wind whistled and whined about Janna's ears. Faintly in the background, she heard the sound of someone crying, and then she landed. She opened her eyes and looked around.

Bookcases and gold embossed wallpaper met her gaze. And Charles. He didn't seem surprised to see her. "Hello," he said. He was lying on his stomach on the floor with a newspaper open in front of him. He rolled over and sat up. "I didn't hear you come in. Have you come to say good-bye?"

"Good-bye?" Janna collapsed onto the floor beside him feeling dizzy.

"You'll come back in the fall, won't you?" Charles went on. "I wonder if you'll see any grasshopper plagues. It says in the paper that the grasshopper menace is serious in the south. But you're going north. Do they get grasshoppers in the north?"

"How should I know?" Janna shuffled uncomfortably in the same threadbare blue dress she had worn the previous day, although it seemed more worn this time, and tighter across her chest.

"How long will it take you to get to your uncle's farm?" Charles asked.

"What are you talking about?" Janna glanced out the window as she spoke. The sunlight on the crabapple tree made the lacy fringe of new leaves glow translucent green. Janna stared. "How did that happen?" she exclaimed. "There were apples on that tree yesterday."

Charles had gone back to his newspaper. "It'll be a couple of months before there are apples." He indicated the article he was reading. "Do you think the Grads will win this time? It says here that the Chicago team is really good. Of course, I think..."

"But yesterday..."

Charles rolled over. "I went to the dentist yesterday. No cavities." He opened his mouth to show her.

"Before that," Janna said. "When we ran away to hide from your Grandma."

Charles grinned. "I hide from my grandma everyday, but I didn't see you yesterday. Speaking of which..." He jumped to his feet as a murmur of voices sounded beyond the door. "I'm supposed to be doing review for exams." He dropped the newspaper and opened a book. "Math," he said.

Janna glanced at the paper on the floor. It was dated May 1934. 1934? How was that possible? But then how was it possible that she was there at all? This time Janna knew she wasn't dreaming.

"I want to be a pilot, so I have to be good at math," Charles went on. "I want to fly like Wop May and Grant McConachie."

"Like who?"

Charles rolled his eyes. "Everybody knows who Wop May is. He was the one being chased by the Red Baron when Roy Brown shot him down. And he's the one who tracked the Mad Trapper of Rat River. Remember? And Grant McConachie is the one who landed his plane on a ten foot beach to rescue that telegrapher."

"Never heard of them."

The library door opened before Charles could express the amazement reflected on his face. "Janna, we moeten gaan." A smell of ammonia and carbolic soap followed the foreign woman into the room. She took her apron off her wide hips and folded it as she spoke. "Je vader wacht."

The words bounced off Janna's ears like pebbles. "I'm sorry," she said. "I don't understand."

The woman frowned. "Ik wil er niet over zeuren, maar we moeten voortmaken. Kom alsjeblieft."

Janna had no idea why everyone, including this woman, seemed to believe they knew each other. "Can't you see," she cried, "that I'm not who you think I am?"

"Is something wrong, Mrs. Vriend?" Charles' grandmother interrupted from the door. Her lips were clamped into a thin line across her narrow face.

Mrs. Vriend shook her head and spoke in English. "No, Mrs. Randolph. We were just leaving."

Janna backed away. No one was going to make her go anywhere. "I'm not leaving."

Mrs. Randolph frowned. "Charles is trying to do his homework."

"Janna was just saying goodbye." Mrs. Vriend stepped forward and grasped Janna's arm with a rough red hand. "Kom nou. We moeten opschieten."

Janna stared at her in astonishment. This time the sounds Mrs. Vriend made settled softly in her ears like snowflakes. They melted and trickled into her consciousness so that she understood what Mrs. Vriend had said. Come now. We have to hurry. "I can't come with you," she protested. Her voice died away as she became aware of the noises coming out of her mouth. She too was speaking the foreign language. She felt a sense of panic.

Mrs. Randolph held out her hand to Mrs. Vriend. "I hope you have a good summer in Neerlandia." She held open the library door. "Come and see me when you come back in the fall. I may still need you."

Holding Janna's arm, Mrs. Vriend guided her down the dimly lit passage towards the kitchen. She picked up a droopy felt hat from the top of a legged, box-like refrigerator. "If we hurry, we'll make the four o'clock streetcar." She opened the back door.

Janna considered bolting back to the library and flinging herself at the painting but when she glanced over her shoulder, Mrs. Randolph was blocking the way. Dazed and confused, Janna trailed out the door and down the path after Mrs. Vriend. Her shoes pinched her toes, and as she crossed the road, gravel squeezed through a hole in the bottom of her sole.

Janna stopped and pulled off her shoe, grateful for a pause in which to think. Her mind was whirling. She couldn't go with Mrs. Vriend; she had to try to get back to the painting in the library.

"I wish we could get some shoes for you," Mrs. Vriend said, resting in the scanty shade of one of the young trees which grew beside the sidewalk. "But that will have to wait until your father gets a job. At least in Neerlandia you'll only need them for Sundays."

The mention of Neerlandia made Janna panic. "I have to go," she said, straightening. "I left . . . " Her mind went blank for a moment. "I left . . . my . . . my locket in the library." She turned to sprint back towards Charles' house but Mrs. Vriend reached out and grabbed Janna's arm.

"There's no time. You know Mr. DeJong is waiting to leave. Mrs. Randolph will keep it for you."

"All right." Desperately Janna came up with another idea. If she lagged behind she could make sure that Mrs. Vriend caught the streetcar and she didn't.

They turned again onto a wide street with tracks down the middle and cyclists weaving between ancient noisy cars with large grille-fronted hoods and poky narrow windshields. Close by, a train whistle hooted. "Hurry!" Mrs. Vriend said, raising her voice above the screech of a streetcar approaching along the middle of the street. She tugged Janna's hand and began to run.

Janna pulled her arm free and slowed to allow a large woman towing a string of children to pass her, hoping to take the opportunity to escape, but the woman, heaving and puffing, slowed too and Janna got caught up in the flow of children. She attempted to bolt in the opposite direction, but a teenage boy wearing floppy pants ran into her and sent her flying towards the streetcar. A man with a cap pulled down over his eyes caught her under her arms and pushed her up the steps. "There you go, lass," he said. Janna found herself swept into the car.

"Do watch where you're going," Mrs. Vriend said, as the car set off with a squeal of steel wheels and a swaying that sent the passengers reeling down the coach.

Janna found a seat beside Mrs. Vriend at the back. She pressed her face against the window and tried not to panic. If she fixed the landmarks in her mind, she should be able to find her way back by following the streetcar tracks. And once she got back to this neighbourhood, she knew her way back to Charles' house.

The streetcar took the same bridge that Dennis had driven her over the day before. The streetcar, however, perched perilously on the top level of the bridge so that the river was a flat blue band far below. Janna felt sick. She looked away from the water and stared instead at the city skyline. It looked very different. There were no glistening glass skyscrapers on the hill above the river; only the domed legislature was familiar.

Janna wondered whether to flee at the next stop, then decided against it. The large woman with all the children spilling over into the aisle was in the way. Janna glanced at the family curiously. They looked exactly like the pictures she had seen of the Depression. The boys' tattered overalls were patched at the knees and the seat, and they were too short, except for those of the barefooted youngest on his mother's lap. His overalls were baggy and too large for him. The little girl had holes in the elbows of her sweater and the lines showed on her dress where the hemline had been let down and let down again.

The streetcar changed direction with a sudden lurch and more grinding and squealing. "I hope the roads to Neerlandia are good," Mrs. Vriend said, clutching the seat in front of her to keep her balance. "And we don't get stuck in the mud like last time. Still, it's kind of Mr. DeJong to take us and perhaps we will get there by lunch time tomorrow. We have to stop on the way in Morinville and Westlock as Mr. DeJong has business."

Janna was concentrating on the direction in which they

were travelling. The streetcar turned again into a major paved thoroughfare. More vintage cars with running boards and mudguards and spare tires attached to their trunks rumbled along beside them. The three-and four-storeyed brick buildings they passed had arched windows and imposing pillared entrances. The streetcar rattled past office blocks and banks with cornices and pilasters, a church, a movie theatre and some food stores. Janna wished she had concentrated more the day before when her uncle had driven her through the city centre. It might have helped her now.

Mrs. Vriend stood up. "Here is our stop."

Janna followed her and the large woman and children out onto the street. The children ran to a dejected man wearing a stained jacket and shabby pants which bagged at his knees.

"Poor souls," Mrs. Vriend said, smoothing her own faded dress. "They look as though they've come from Saskatchewan. Well, they won't find things much better here, and we should know. Oh dear..." Mrs. Vriend hurried forward as the little girl in front of her tripped.

Janna seized her opportunity. Ducking behind a smartly dressed woman in a slim navy dress with a white hat and gloves, Janna fled down the sidewalk.

"Janna!" she heard Mrs. Vriend call behind her a moment later. She didn't look back. She dodged into the doorway of a tobacconist and peered down the street. She could see Mrs. Vriend stop a man in a baggy pin-striped suit and fedora. The man shook his head.

Quelling guilt, Janna hid herself behind a portly gentleman whose pants reached his armpits. She shuffled another block up the street behind him. Then she ran as fast as she was able, stumbling sometimes over uneven ground, dodging ladies pushing baby carriages, scruffy boys, men in suits with hats and newspapers, and men just standing on street corners with glazed expressions on their faces. She got lost only once, but she asked directions to the high bridge from a grubby boy in breeches and then she found her way again. After that, although her toes were blistered raw and her breathing was ragged, she followed the tracks in the middle of the road and limped, hot and perspiring, to Charles' neighbourhood.

His street was easy to find. She hesitated as she hobbled down the sidewalk, wondering whether to try and creep into the house as she had done the previous time or whether to knock. She decided to knock. If she crept in and was discovered, Charles' miserable grandmother would probably have her arrested. She reached to her neck and undid the clasp of her locket. She would say that she had left it in the library.

She wiped her sweaty palms on her skirt before she lifted the shiny brass sailing ship knocker on the front door and tapped it gingerly. Nothing happened. She knocked again, more loudly, and strained her ears for the sound of footsteps. But she heard only the echo of the knocker inside the house, the song of a robin in the bare branches of the lilacs, a car slowing down on the street behind her, and a car door slamming. She was about to turn, despairing when, finally, she caught the tap of footsteps down the passage. The front door flew open.

Mrs. Randolph's eyebrows arched. "Yes?"

Janna struggled to shift the gears in her brain so that she spoke the right language. "I . . . er . . . think I left my locket in the library."

"Wait," Mrs. Randolph said. "I will ask Charles to look." She closed the door in Janna's face.

"But I . . ." Janna called, but she was interrupted before she had time to complete her sentence.

"Janna!" She turned to see a big-shouldered blond man with a thunderous expression on his face storming down the path towards her. Parked behind him was an antiquated pick-up. Mrs. Vriend was in the front and a freckle-faced boy with spiky blond hair was leaning over fence boards built around the box. He grinned and made a face.

Janna backed away as the blond man approached, but he reached out and grabbed her shoulder. "Come with me," he said in the foreign language.

"No," Janna yelled, struggling to free herself.

"Don't speak to your father like that." The man steered her forcibly down the path. "How can you be so thoughtless?" he asked angrily. "Your mother has been worried sick."

"Charles can't find your locket," Mrs. Randolph called from the front door.

The man doffed his cap and then scowled at Janna. "Get in the truck."

Janna had no choice but to comply.

Chapter Five

Janna sat in the cab crushed between Mrs. Vriend's sprawling hips and the driver, Mr. DeJong's bony elbows, with the smell of dust, sweat, and pigs in the back of the truck in her nostrils. She stared out the window numb with shock.

"You must cheer up, Janna," Mrs. Vriend said, putting her arm around Janna's shoulder. "I know you don't want to go to Neerlandia but once we get there and you're with Sara, it won't be as bad as you think."

Janna didn't answer. The dust billowing from under the wheels as the truck jolted along the dusty gravel ruts stuck in her throat and made her feel as though she were choking. "Besides," Mrs. Vriend went on, "you know we don't have much choice. We are fortunate that Oom Klaas can use us on the farm this summer; otherwise, we'd have to go on relief. And you know how much your father would hate that."

Janna grimaced at the word father. Her own father had

never yelled at her the way Mr. Vriend had. "Don't make that face," Mrs. Vriend said, glancing behind her towards the box of the truck where Mr. Vriend and the boy, Piet, were cramped under canvas between cardboard boxes, cream cans and pigs. "He was only angry because he was concerned about you. I know your locket is special, but you shouldn't have run off like that. Your father has had enough to worry about lately."

Janna began to cough. There was dust in her mouth, her nostrils, her hair and her clothing. If only she could have a drink or take a shower. She closed her eyes and imagined the feeling of cold water spurting over her body.

But there was no shower that day. There wasn't even a bathroom. They spent the night with a farmer in Morinville, a friend of Mr. DeJong's, and there was only an outhouse out back with an old Eaton's catalogue hanging on the door for toilet paper. To sleep, Janna shared a spiky straw mattress in the loft of the farmer's house with Mrs. Vriend. She lay stiffly on the prickly bedding listening to rustling and the patter of feet that had to be mice — or rats, and Mrs. Vriend's heavy breathing. She tried to crush the rising panic she felt and to make some sense of what was happening. Why did the Vriends think she was their daughter? And if they did have a daughter, where was she? And how was Janna going to get back to Omie's?

The sun was a gold sliver on the horizon when Mrs. Vriend roused Janna the next morning. Janna was too tired to protest, or to eat the slabs of dry bread spread with pale lard which they had for breakfast.

"Are you going back to Edmonton tonight, Mr. DeJong?" Mrs. Vriend asked as they squeezed back into the truck.

Janna's ears pricked up. If he were, she could hide in the box of the truck and get a ride back with him.

"Not tonight," Mr. DeJong replied. "My business in Westlock will take some time so it will be too late by the time we get to Neerlandia. I'm taking the pigs to the Groots so I'll spend the night with them and leave early tomorrow."

Janna slumped back in her seat. She would have to wait another night. She stared out the window at the scenery they were passing. There was little to see: a few isolated log or frame farmhouses, large hip-roofed barns and ploughed fields. After Westlock, the ploughed fields gave way to trees: tangled poplars and willows spiked with silver birch, dark green spruce and tamarack.

"It's not much farther now," Mr. DeJong said later, as the road grew bumpier and bumpier. "Corduroy roads," he added cheerfully as Janna's teeth rattled in her mouth.

They arrived as the sun was sinking and the silhouetted trees cast dark shadows over a small, square, two-storey log house with a peaked roof and dormer windows. A barefooted girl and two smaller boys came running to meet them as the Vriends tumbled out of the truck. Janna hung back, a feeling of isolation sweeping round her like a cold wind, as the two families became a tangle of affectionate embraces and cheerful greetings.

"Aren't you going to say hello to your uncle?" A wiry, dark-haired man took Janna's shoulders and held her at arm's-length. "Ah, you have grown. You are already a young woman like my Sara."

"Oh Pa!" the barefooted girl said. She grinned at Janna. "Let's go inside. You are sharing my room."

Janna followed the girl inside into the warm amber light of a flickering oil lamp.

"Stay out of the way!" Mr. Vriend said as he and Oom Klaas staggered in behind them carrying a domed steamer trunk.

"This is heavy." Oom Klaas lowered it to the floor. "What have you got in here?"

"Mother's china," Mrs. Vriend answered. "I didn't want to leave it with our neighbours."

Oom Klaas put his arm around Mrs. Vriend and smiled at her. "Still feeling homesick?"

"Not all the time." She smiled back. "Not now. I'm glad to be here with you."

"And I'm glad you are here," Klaas answered. "It's been hard for the children since Anna died, especially for Sara." He turned to Mr. Vriend. "And I will be very grateful for your help in the fields."

"How are things going on the farm?" Mr. Vriend asked.

"God willing, it will be a good year," Oom Klaas replied. "I've seeded ten acres and I've managed to clear another two. But prices are still down. It's not worth trying to sell the pigs. And nobody wants calves. We had two born this spring and I slaughtered both of them. I couldn't afford to waste milk on them. The cream cheque is our only income."

"Come upstairs to my room," Sara said, unmoved by her father's conversation. "I'll get a candle."

Mr. Vriend's voice followed them up the steep, narrow, wooden staircase. "You should see what it is like now in Edmonton. There are some people living in shacks made of cardboard and digging in the garbage cans for food."

"Well, here God has been gracious and we have enough to eat and a roof over our heads."

Their voices were cut off as Sara closed her bedroom door behind them. She put the candle on a tall chest of drawers. "You can put your things in there or in the wardrobe." She opened the door of the wardrobe which had only two dresses hanging in it. "There's lots of room." She swung the door closed and leapt onto a high bed with a log frame, settling cross-legged on the patchwork cover. "And now we can talk." She leaned forward and took Janna's hand, pulling her closer. "You must tell me everything that's happened since we last saw each other."

Janna perched on the edge of the bed. The familiar sense of unreality made her feel faint. Even Sara believed she was someone else, and it was going to be much more difficult dealing with her than it had been coping with Mr. and Mrs. Vriend. "You start," she said.

Sara was happy to do so. She chatted on about a boy she liked at school, about school, about church, about the girls' society at church, and about a number of people she thought Janna knew.

Janna tried to nod and laugh when she was expected to but her laughter sounded forced and strained. She got off the bed and stared at herself in the mirror above Sara's dresser. She hardly recognized the face that met her gaze. Her hair was longer, her cheeks thinner, and yet it was her face. Or was it? Janna felt sick with confusion. Was it possible that she had somehow changed places with the Vriends' daughter because she looked like her and had the same name? And if she had, was the other Janna now with her mother and Roddy?

Sara interrupted her thoughts. "You're not listening."

"Yes, I am," Janna lied. She turned to the window. "Do the Groots live close by?"

Sara looked surprised. "They still have the next quarter section." She joined Janna at the small window and pointed. "Over there." A pale moon covered with wisps of ghostly clouds gave faint light. As far as Janna could see there were only dark trees stirring in the wind. An owl hooted eerily. Fear twisted in her stomach. How would she find her way?

She tossed restlessly that night beside Sara's soft curled shape, afraid to sleep in case she didn't wake in time to creep out, and dreaming over and over again that she had found her way to the Groots only to wake to the crushing discovery that the journey still lay ahead.

It rained during the night and the patter of raindrops on the roof finally lulled her into unconsciousness. She dreamed then that she was trapped in Mr. DeJong's truck, jolting and juddering along the dusty track farther and farther away from home. She could feel her body shaking.

"Janna! Wake up!" Sara was kneeling on the bed beside her, shaking her shoulder. "We have to find the cows."

Janna opened her eyes a slit. The sky through the window was deep blue velvet. "What?"

"The cows. Are you coming?"

Janna opened her eyes wide and jerked upright. "What time is it?"

"Around five. The clock is downstairs." Sara climbed off the bed and began to dress.

"Five! In the morning!" At least Mr. DeJong couldn't have left yet. Janna jumped out of bed and began rummaging through the few pieces of underwear Mrs. Vriend had packed in her drawer. She pulled out a pair of baggy cotton bloomers and shivered. "It's cold. Do you always wake up this early?"

Sara nodded. "Of course. I have to find the cows and milk them while the boys get water for the house and the pigs."

Janna opened the closet and pulled out the clean dress she had hung there. "Why don't you do it later?"

Sara looked puzzled. "Because I have to separate the milk

and feed the pigs. You shouldn't wear that dress," she added as Janna began to pull the clean dress over her head. "You'll need it for church tomorrow." She shook Janna's old dirty dress until a cloud of dust motes glittered like flecks of gold in the morning light. "Wear this one."

Mrs. Vriend was in the kitchen bent over a shiny black wood stove with a silver chimney that went up the wall and across the ceiling. "Good morning girls," she said, stretching for more kindling from the box that stood by the oven. "Coffee?" She straightened up and poured them each a cup from the pot on the stove and added a generous amount of milk.

Sara took a sip and made a face. "Barley, you mean. Are we out of sugar?"

"We must be thankful for what we have," Mrs. Vriend said, giving Sara a kiss on the top of her head.

Janna wrapped her hands around the warm mug of liquid and followed Sara outside. The cool air smelled of damp earth and new rain. Rays of sunlight stretched above the treetops and the sky was streaked with apricot gold. Plumes of mist curled round the trees.

"Come on," Sara said, heading towards scrub some distance from the house. "You go to the slough. I'll go to the creek. The cows are usually in one of those places."

"Why don't you just lock them up?" Janna asked, running after Sara into long wet grass.

Sara gave her a strange look. "They have to eat."

"Oh." The answer didn't make sense to Janna, but she didn't pursue it. She had more urgent matters to concentrate on. "Is the slough close to your neighbours?" she asked as the wet grass slapped her shins. "I . . . " Her mind searched frantically for an explanation. "I . . . just wanted to give Mr. DeJong a message to take back to Edmonton about the locket I lost. Ouch!" A branch from a bush swung back and whipped Janna across the thighs. She stepped backwards into a tree. A shower of drops rained down on her head.

"They're in the same direction," Sara said, laughing. "But the Groots are a little farther than the slough. Since you've forgotten everything, you'd better wait and I'll take you there after we've milked the cows." She indicated a narrow path through the grass which split into two directions. "Stay on the cow trail. It goes in a circle so you can't get lost."

The bush grew denser and Janna stumbled over protruding roots and the thorny branches of brilliant pink wild roses. Her legs were scratched and bleeding but she blundered on, straining her senses for any sign of human habitation ahead. However, the scrub was too thick to see anything and all she could hear was the call of birds and the hum of bees in the fragrant white blossoms of the choke cherries and saskatoons, and in the bluebells and white fairy bells which grew under the dogwoods and high bush cranberries along the path.

And then the scrub thinned. The ground grew damp

under Janna's feet and the grass grew longer, new green spears sprouting through dead brown straw. Off the path, dead cattail stalks choked stagnant brown puddles which smelled of rotting vegetation. Ducks flew overhead and their cries echoed in the stillness. Janna realized she must be getting close to the slough. That meant she was also getting close to the neighbours. She quickened her step over the squelchy ground.

As the path turned, Janna could see the slough ahead. Wisps of steam rose from the dark surface of the water and ducks glided back and forth glinting iridescent green in the sunlight. Farther, in the shallows, she could make out dark shapes amongst the cattails, rocks perhaps.

A spiral of smoke on the horizon to the left of the slough gave her hope. Perhaps it was coming from the neighbours. Her sodden shoes sank into mud which seeped through the holes and oozed between her toes. As she stopped to pull off her shoes, she glanced at the rocks she had noticed earlier. Closer now, she noticed they had horns at one end. Horns! That meant she had found the cows. Janna groaned. "Go home cows," she shouted. One of the cows lowed mournfully in reply, but none of them moved. There was something peculiar about the way they were sitting, or perhaps kneeling, in the water. "Hey cows!" she shouted again. "It's time to go home!" She waved her arms encouragingly. "Go home!"

Janna shrugged. If they didn't want to go, she couldn't

make them. As she stepped forward, her bare foot sank into mud up to her knee. She struggled to free it from the clinging squelch and realized suddenly what had happened to the cows. They must be stuck in the mud. One of the cows mooed. The rest stared pleadingly at Janna.

She gritted her teeth. She couldn't help them. She had to get back to Edmonton. She floundered forward: the mud was almost like quicksand. It was no wonder the cows were stuck. It occurred to her that if Sara didn't get to them in time, they might die. She glanced back at them. Dark brown eyes met hers. She stared ahead at the wisp of smoke, and then, with a heavy heart, started retracing her steps toward the house. Perhaps Mr. DeJong was leaving later in the day.

Chapter Six

By the time Janna found Sara, who was ambling along the path holding a bunch of wild flowers to her nose, mud was caked between Janna's toes and under her fingernails. It clotted on her shins and crusted down her legs and skirt. Sara laughed when she saw Janna. "What happened to you?"

Janna was too tired to retort. She bent over and rested her hands on her knees to catch her breath. "The cows," she panted. "They're stuck in the slough."

"Oh no!" Sara dropped her flowers. "We've got to be quick. The water is so cold that they'll catch a chill and we'll lose them all. I'll get my father. He'll pull them out with a horse." She started to run down the path. "You go to the house and clean up."

But Janna didn't go back to the house. She led Mr. Vriend and Oom Klaas to the bog where she had seen the cows and held the horses with Sara as the men edged precariously along planks over the muskeg until they were able to slide loops of rope over the cows' heads. Then the horses pulled and strained and the cows rose from the slime like creatures from a horror movie.

"I think we got there just in time," Oom Klaas said as they all sat around the wooden kitchen table an hour later, "for which we can thank God, and Janna and Sara." He closed the big black Bible from which he had just read a chapter and put it beside the blue and white dishes on the dresser.

Mr. Vriend nodded and passed Janna a plate of warm pancakes.

"I helped too," the freckled-faced boy, Piet, protested.

Janna was too tired to respond. She huddled on the chair closest to the wood fire in the stove in an old patched dress of Sara's and glanced at the clock on the top shelf of the dresser. It was only 8:00 a.m. At home she wouldn't even be awake at this time. At home . . . Janna jerked herself awake. She had forgotten all about Mr. DeJong. Perhaps there was still time to catch him.

"Good morning. Good morning," a hearty voice broke into her thoughts. A barrel-chested man with a bushy moustache shook hands with Mr. and Mrs. Vriend and proffered a jar of ruby-coloured jam. "From my wife," he said. "With her welcome."

"I was going to bring Janna to your house when we had finished breakfast," Sara said to the man. "She wants to give Mr. DeJong a message to take back to Edmonton about her locket."

"Mr. DeJong left about half an hour ago," Mr. Groot said.

"But if you like, I'll take your message. I have to go to Edmonton next week."

"Can I come?" Janna blurted. "Then I could..."

"Gerrit walks to Edmonton," Oom Klaas said, shaking his head and rolling his eyes. "He doesn't believe in the modern methods of transportation."

Mr. Groot laughed. "God gave me a good pair of legs. Walking takes awhile, but I get there safely. So, if you have a letter, I will be happy to deliver it for you."

Defeated, Janna took the pencil Mrs. Vriend gave her and tried to think of what to write. In the end her letter was very short.

Dear Charles,

Thank you for looking for my locket for me. As I have not yet found it, I hope to come back and see you sometime and look for it again. We are in Neerlandia on my uncle's farm. This morning the cows sank in the muskeg and we had to drag them out. It was an interesting experience.

Yours sincerely,
Janna

She sealed it in an envelope. "I'd like to walk to Edmonton with you," she said. "It would make me fit."

Oom Klaas laughed. "We have a lot of things to do here on the farm that will make you fit. Sara will show you."

"He means chores," Sara said with a grimace. "Come on. Let's get started."

"And we must get back to the fields," Mr. Vriend said, standing up. "Clearing is slow work. Some of those stumps won't budge."

"One day, God willing, I'll be able to buy a tractor," Oom Klaas said, as he and Mr. Vriend and the visitor walked out the back door. "But for now I just keep thanking God that the horses haven't gone lame and that the harnesses have lasted another year."

"Chores?" Janna said. "We've already done chores. I mean, we found the cows and then you milked them and separated the milk."

"The pigs have to be fed for one thing."

"You girls go and collect the eggs," Mrs. Vriend said, as she cleared the dishes from the table. "You boys had better get back to the garden."

"But Moeke," Piet complained to his mother. "The girls always get the easy work."

"Don't you worry about Sara and Janna, Piet," Mrs. Vriend said, tousling his head. "You do what you have to do. Now I'd like all of you out of here. I want to wash this floor and then I'm going to bake some bread for tomorrow."

"Where are the eggs?" Janna asked as she followed Sara barefoot from the house.

Sara frowned. "This morning you didn't know how to milk the cows, and now you don't know where the eggs are. How can you have forgotten? It's not that long since you were here. What's wrong with you?"

Janna was tempted to confide in Sara and tell her what

had happened, but no one would believe her. "It's hard to explain," she said. "I've just had so many things happen lately that I guess my brain got scrambled."

Sara didn't look convinced. "The chicken house is over there. Past the garden." She pointed to a low log structure beside a strawstack. Several chickens and some chicks scratched and pecked at the dirt nearby. "Do you remember our rooster?" she asked as they walked past the large fenced garden. It had already been ploughed and Janna could see green shoots poking through the black earth.

Janna shook her head in answer to Sara's question.

"Well, you will soon." As Sara spoke a stately golden bird with a long plumed tail separated himself from the hens and strutted over to them. Sara waved the syrup pail she was carrying at him. "Go away!"

The bird arched its neck and scratched at the ground. Janna took a step backwards. The rooster advanced.

"Don't let him see that you're afraid," Sara said. She waved the pail at the rooster again. "Go away, you mean old thing!" But the rooster had his little round red eyes fixed on Janna's bare feet. He side-stepped Sara and charged at Janna flapping wide gold wings. Janna, taken by surprise, took to her heels with the rooster, followed by Sara, in pursuit. The boys, who were perched on the garden fence, roared with laughter.

"What is wrong with you?" Sara demanded after she finally swiped the rooster with the pail and sent him into a sulky retreat.

"There's nothing wrong with me," Janna snapped, trying to muster her shattered dignity. She glared at the boys and snatched the pail from Sara's grip. Marching towards the chicken house, she flailed it wildly in the direction of the sullen rooster. "Come near me again and I'll knock your head off, you evil bird," she muttered threateningly, glad the rooster was too far away to hear her heart pounding.

Janna blinked as she stooped to enter the chicken house. It was dark inside apart from sunlight glinting through chinks between the logs.

"If there's nothing wrong with you," Sara demanded, from behind her, "why are you being so secretive?"

"What do you mean?"

"You know what I mean," Sara said. She took the pail and began scooping eggs from the hay-filled ledge. "You haven't told me what's been happening in Edmonton, or about losing your locket, or about the boy you sent a message to, or about anything."

Janna shrugged. "There's nothing to tell."

Sara banged down the pail. "That's what I mean," she said. "You're being a snob. You're even talking differently. Just because you live in the city, you think you're swanky. Well, what I think is..."

"No," Janna interrupted. "That's not it." She shuffled her feet in the straw. "Look, if I told you the truth, you'd never believe me."

Sara looked interested. "Try me," she said.

Janna's fingers tightened round the warm brown egg she

was holding. "I'm not really who you think I am," she began. "My name is Janna Sanderson, not Janna Vriend and I come from the future. I think Janna Vriend and I have changed places. It's because of a painting in my grandma's house. I was staring at it and . . ."

Sara bumped her head on the low roof as she straightened her back. "All right!" she said angrily. "So you don't want to talk to me. That's fine by me. I don't want to talk to you either." She picked up the pail of eggs and stalked out the chicken house.

"Sara, wait!" Janna ran after her. "I told you you wouldn't believe me. But please," she begged. "Tell me one thing. How can I get to Edmonton?"

Sara glared at her. "Go back," she said. "I don't care. You can go on the cream truck on Monday."

Janna wanted to ask Sara where she could find the cream truck and what time it left, but Sara's angry expression forbade any further questioning so she trailed after her to the house in silence.

Mrs. Vriend handed them a pail of skim milk. "Janna can take the milk to the piglets."

"They're in the strawstack, in case you've forgotten that as well," Sara muttered to Janna with a scathing expression.

Piet and the boys were pulling weeds in the garden as Janna set off in search of the strawstack. Piet made a face when he saw her. Janna ignored him. Jakob, Sara's brother, leaned over and whispered something in Piet's ear. Both boys laughed.

Janna stared stonily ahead. She would only have to put up with them for another two days and then she could go back home to her own brother. Thoughts of Roddy brought painful pangs of homesickness for her family. She wondered what her mother and Roddy were doing. Perhaps they liked the new Janna better. Janna wished that she hadn't been so rude the night she left.

When Janna neared the strawstack the piglets popped out of the straw like little pink gophers. She put down the pail she was carrying and tried to grab one.

"You mustn't do that," an anxious voice behind her said. It was Willie, Sara's six-year-old brother, running towards her. He picked up the pail and poured the pigs' milk into a trough.

"I'll be gentle," Janna said, edging nearer to the little piglets who were grunting and snuffling over the trough.

Willie shook his head and pointed a muddy finger at a pair of beady eyes and a large snout protruding from the straw. "The mother is watching."

"Hey, Willie, you get back to the garden and finish your job!" Jakob loped over to them and gave Willie a threatening glare.

"Janna was trying to hold a piglet," Willie said, as he scurried back to the garden.

Jakob turned to Janna. "So you want to hold a piglet?" Behind him, behind the fence, Piet was grinning from ear to ear.

Janna stared suspiciously from one to the other.

"You have to be careful when you hold piglets," Jakob went on, stifling a laugh. "They wriggle. And they squeal. Like this." He stepped right up to Janna and imitated the squeals of the piglets.

As Janna held her hands over her ears, Jakob bolted, still squealing, and scrambled onto the roof of the chicken house. Out of the corner of her eye, Janna caught sight of the sow, the size of a bulldozer, bursting from the strawstack.

"Run!" Willie screamed.

Janna ran, the sow pounding after her.

"No," Jakob yelled. "This way! Not to the house You won't make it!" His voice was tinged with fear.

It was too late to change direction. Janna could feel the vibrations of the sow's thundering feet. As she glanced over her shoulder, she could see large bared teeth. She could almost feel the sow's hot breath on her ankles. She'd never make it to the door of the house, but perhaps she could make it to the window.

With all the energy she had left, she dived through the open window and crashed on the floor in the kitchen. As she skidded across the linoleum into a 100lb sack of flour, she looked back. The window blacked out. The sow dived in after her.

Janna screamed and ran from the room, banging the door closed behind her.

"You were lucky that bag of flour was there," Mrs. Vriend said later as she and Janna dusted flour from the walls, the shelves, the dishes, the table, the chairs, the stove and the floor of the kitchen. "If that sow hadn't had that to attack, she might have broken through the kitchen door after you."

Mr. Vriend shook his head. "I don't understand how you could be so foolish. You know you never try to pick up the piglets when the mother is there. What's come over you?"

"Well, no harm's done. I suppose we should be grateful for that." Mrs. Vriend gave Janna a reassuring hug.

"No harm but a bag of flour lost," Mr. Vriend snorted as he put his hat on to leave. "And time wasted that could have been better spent elsewhere. Piet has had what he deserves, but I don't know what to do about you, Janna. You're almost fourteen."

"I'll deal with Janna," said Mrs. Vriend, wiping a streak of flour from her cheek with a powdery hand. She took Janna's arm and sat her down on one of the high ladder-back chairs round the table.

"We'll forget about the pig," she said as she crossed to the stove and poured two cups of barley coffee. "You haven't been yourself lately. Something is bothering you. Why don't you tell me what's wrong, Janna? It must be more than your lost locket." She placed the coffee on the table and settled on a chair. "Is there anything I can do to help?"

Janna didn't know what to say. She leaned her elbows on the thick patterned table cover and buried her head in her hands. "I'm sorry about the mess."

"That's not what's troubling you," Mrs. Vriend said.

Janna wished she could tell her. "I feel lonely sometimes. I'm homesick," she answered finally. It was the truth.

Mrs. Vriend patted Janna's hand. "My poor little love. These last few years have been hard on you — leaving Holland and then going back and forth between here and Edmonton, making friends and then leaving them. No wonder you feel homesick. But eventually your father will get a job. He has a good education, you know. When we settle somewhere, you will be able to put down your roots. You are young enough yet that you will be able to do it." She paused and stared at the lace curtains fluttering at the window with a sudden far away look on her face.

Janna saw her expression and recognized it. "Are you lonely?" she asked.

Mrs. Vriend smiled. "Sometimes. I miss Oma and my sisters. And the flowers at home. Do you remember the flowers in spring time, Janna? No, you were too young to notice flowers. When we first came to Canada I thought it would become home, but now I know I am too old to leave the past behind altogether."

"I'd like to go back to Edmonton," Janna said. She thought of the events of the day: of struggling through the muskeg, of being chased by the pig, of the boys' laughter and Sara's anger. "I don't belong here."

Mrs. Vriend smiled and reached out for Janna's hand. "We are like fish swimming in two ponds, but you always belong with those who love you."

Her words brought tears to Janna's eyes. Mrs. Vriend stroked her hand. "God does not give you trials without giving you the strength to bear them. And don't worry, we won't stay in Neerlandia for long. Your father is too impatient to be a farmer." She got up and opened the oven door. A warm smell of baking flooded the room. "The baking powder biscuits are ready," she said. "Would you like one? That might help to make you feel better. Then you'd better go and help Sara finish the chores."

Sara giggled when she saw Janna. "I'm sorry to laugh," she said. "But that sow chasing you was the funniest thing I ever saw in my life." She reached out and touched Janna's arm. "And when Jakob told me what happened, I realized that you couldn't be pretending to have forgotten. I think you must have lost your memory."

"Maybe that's it," Janna agreed. She was relieved that Sara was talking to her again. At least she would be able to find out about the cream truck.

Sara giggled again. "You do look a sight. Thank goodness today is bath day."

"You have a bath!" Janna was delighted. But she was less impressed when she saw the metal tub that Oom Klaas placed in front of the oven that evening.

"You can bath first," Sara said as Mrs. Vriend filled the tub with steaming water from the reservoir on the stove.

"Here?" Janna asked in disbelief. "In that? Don't you put a curtain around it or anything?"

"What for?" Sara handed Janna a bar of soap. "I made this soap myself, out of pig lard."

Janna wrinkled her nose as she took the bar of soap and stepped into the water. She wrinkled her nose at dinner time too when she realized they were eating a rabbit that Mr. Vriend had shot, but she was hungry and shovelled it into her mouth with the bottled beets, carrots and turnips which Mrs. Vriend had taken from the cellar underneath the kitchen floor.

That night, although she was clean and full, Janna lay awake again thinking about the strangeness of what was happening to her. She hoped that Roddy wouldn't love Janna Vriend more than he loved her.

Chapter Seven

"Sunday's my favourite day," Sara said as she pulled her starched Sunday dress over her head. "No school and no chores! And I love seeing everyone at church."

"Mmm." Janna was distracted. She was thinking about how to bring up the subject of the cream truck without making Sara angry again. "So what happens on Mondays?" she asked.

"Are you ready to go, girls?" Mrs. Vriend interrupted cheerfully. She was wearing a blue floral dress that brought out the colour in her eyes. For the first time Janna noticed how pretty she was. Mrs. Vriend pulled on her gloves and checked her hat in Sara's mirror. "We don't want to be late."

The family piled into a wagon while Mr. Vriend, whistling, hitched up the horses. Janna sat beside Mrs. Vriend as they bounced and bumped through the clear spring morning. A soft breeze caressed her hair and filled her nostrils with the smell of clover and pine needles. "How does the cream get to Edmonton?" she asked, over the creaking and groaning of the wagon wheels and the clop of the horses' hooves on the dirt road.

"The truck comes for it," Mrs. Vriend answered. "You know," she went on, "on beautiful days like this, I think we shouldn't be riding to church. We should walk so that we can breathe in the beauty of the morning."

"And what time does it leave?" Janna asked.

"Early. Before breakfast. And if we left early, we could enjoy the walk to church."

"So where does it leave from?" Janna persisted.

Mrs. Vriend wasn't listening. "The Groots walk sometimes. We could go with them."

Janna gave up. She would have to ask Sara. She waited impatiently through the hymns which resounded through the cool dark church, and through the dominie's long message. Sara passed the time whispering to a friend beside her and trying to attract the attention of a boy who sat with the men on the opposite side of the church.

When they were finally released from the hard wooden benches and spilled out from the cool dim church into the bright sunlit day, there was still no opportunity to question Sara. The family joined another family from the church for crusty home-made bread and thick vegetable soup.

"The Vinks have a *radio,*" Sara told Janna after Mr. Vink had given thanks at the end of the meal. "I wish we had one. Sometimes we come here and listen to *Amos and Andy* but on Sundays we have to listen to Mr. Aberhart's sermon."

Janna racked her brains. "Wasn't . . . I mean . . . isn't Aberhart the Premier of Alberta? Wasn't he the one who promised everybody money?"

Sara shook her head. "Oh no," she said. "He's not the premier. He's a preacher and a teacher. Pa says Mr. Aberhart is teaching everybody about a new system of economics that will end the Depression."

"*Everybody* knows Mr. Brownlea is our premier," Piet said smugly.

"Not for much longer, I hope," their host put in before Janna could think of a scathing reply. "Next elections I'm voting Social Credit. I think that Mr. Aberhart is right about the Douglas system. That's what will get us on our feet again."

Oom Klaas nodded. "Maybe so, but I think that fellow, that former Secretary of Agriculture from the United States, has a point. He said in the paper last week that if the United States would get right spiritually, it could snap out of the Depression in ninety days."

"It'll take more than that," Mr. Vriend muttered. "Part of the problem is that too many people want something for nothing. Did you read about the relief workers' strike? Now they expect to be paid for being idle."

"Perhaps you are being too harsh," Oom Klaas said. "Those people would work if they could find a job."

"I can't find a job, but I don't lie around all day expecting someone else to feed my family," Mr. Vriend retorted. "I won't go on relief."

Mrs. Vriend fanned her face with a table napkin. "It's

close enough in here without you two arguing," she said. "Can't you talk about something more cheerful on Sundays?"

"Did you read about that baby girl they rescued from that auger hole?" Mrs. Vink asked. "She was down there for one and a half hours but they managed to get her out and she was fine."

Sara looked bored. "Come," she whispered. "Let's go. I'll ask if we can turn on the radio."

But Janna shook her head. She had caught another snatch of the men's conversation and she wanted to hear the rest. "...hoping to send some hogs into Edmonton tomorrow," Mr. Vink said. "Art says he'll take them with the cream. I hope I manage to catch them all before he gets here."

"You'll have plenty of time," Mr. Vriend replied. "He never gets to us before seven."

Janna wanted to shout her delight out loud. She had the answer to her question. The truck came to pick up the cream at seven o'clock in the morning. This time she would be ready.

Janna scarcely slept that night for fear she wouldn't wake in time. But the sun was not yet up when she eased herself out of bed. Through the window she could see the first pearly glow of sunrise in the morning dark sky and hear the strident cheeps from a nest of newly hatched barn swallows under the eaves.

By the time she slipped quietly out the back door, shafts of light reached above the horizon and etched the trees in gold. It had rained again in the night and raindrops hung like diamonds in the branches of the spruce by the house. In the distance, the rooster opened his throat and drowned the chatter of the blackbirds. Janna scurried to the barn and took shelter behind it. The barn was close to the well and she would be able to see the cream truck arrive and assess the right moment to board it.

She watched Oom Klaas come to the well and haul up cans of cream from the cool dark depth, and she saw Sara head in the direction of the cow trail holding a thick slice of bread. Piet and Willie came out of the house next. Piet was teasing the younger boy and ruffling his hair as Willie ducked and protested. Jakob emerged with an axe and began to chop a block of wood from the woodpile outside the back door and the cows, minus Sara, appeared from the trees and ambled towards the barn. Still the truck didn't come.

Janna watched Piet pour water into the trough for the horses, and Oom Klaas lure the horses with grain so that he could harness them. It looked as though they were ready to go out to clear more land. Did that mean the cream truck wasn't coming? But finally a battered old truck sputtered into view.

It was the same kind in which Janna and the Vriends had travelled to Neerlandia: a rectangular cab with large mudguards and a running board and a box enclosed by widely spaced wooden planks like a horse fence.

Oom Klaas tied the horses to the well and strolled over to greet Mr. Fisher. "Wheat's looking good," Janna heard Mr. Fisher say as he got out of the truck. "It must be up six inches."

Oom Klaas nodded and heaved a can of cream into the box. "Rain came just in time after that dry spell. Feel sorry for those poor devils in the south, though."

Janna's heart raced. How could she get on the truck without being seen? There was only one possibility. Keeping her head low, she crept to the passenger side of the truck as the two men loaded the rest of the cream cans and stealthily mounted the running board. She grabbed the door handle and ducked her head. If she crouched, Mr. Fisher wouldn't be able to see her.

Janna clung on as the truck jolted forward and gained speed. She felt as though she was being scrambled as they rumbled over ridged corduroy roads. She closed her eyes as the front wheel hit a muddy pot hole and dirt spattered over her face and clothes. She didn't see the next pot hole coming. The wheel dropped, spun, sprayed mud, and stuck. Mr. Fisher leapt out the truck and strode round to the passenger side. His eyes widened in surprise as he saw Janna, and then he laughed. "Hoping to catch a ride to school, were you?"

Janna wiped a chunk of mud off her face. There was only one more tactic she could try. "I'd like a ride to Edmonton," she said.

Mr. Fisher guffawed with laughter. "You can't go anywhere looking like that. You look like you've got a bad case of mud measles. Come on, get in. I'll take you home."

Janna slumped in the truck beside him. She looked at her mud speckled clothing and legs without emotion. Her whole world had collapsed.

Mrs. Vriend was bent over a tub of steaming water, her face red and beaded with sweat, when Janna was ignominiously dropped back at the house. Tendrils of damp hair curled out of the scarf Mrs. Vriend had wrapped around her head. She shook her head in disbelief when she saw Janna. "You'd better clean yourself up," she said. "You know you have to leave for school in a few minutes."

Janna was still stunned when she left for school a short time later clutching a syrup pail containing four thick slices of bread spread with bacon fat and home-made cottage cheese, and a nickel for a scribbler. "Take care of that money," Mrs. Vriend warned her as they set off. Filled with despair, Janna lagged behind Sara, who was holding Willie's hand and talking about tadpoles. Jakob and Piet had already raced off ahead of them.

Piet gave a shout. "Squirrel! Bet you I can catch it."

"I've got my slingshot. Let me shoot it!" Jakob cried. But Piet had already taken off in pursuit of the squirrel, clambering up the trunk of a spruce tree.

"You'll never get it now!" Jakob yelled. "You're too slow."

"Am not! I let it get away," Piet slithered along the branch of the tree and as it bent beneath his weight, he slid to the branch below and the one below that, until he was sliding down the tree, whooping as he went.

"You'll get dirty for school," Sara shouted as Jakob followed Piet up another tree.

School! That was all Janna needed to complete her misery. Ahead of them, a small white building loomed.

"Come on," Sara said, leading her through an entrance choked with lunch pails and wood stacked against the walls. "This is the girls' cloakroom. You can leave your lunch here."

"Welcome to our class," the teacher said to Janna and Piet. As he spoke in English Janna could feel the gears shifting in her mind. He pointed at a double desk with ornate curved metal legs behind the pot bellied stove in the centre of the room. "You may sit beside your cousin, Janna. Now, after we have said the Lord's Prayer I want grade sixes and sevens to get on with the seat work on the board. Grade fives, take out your readers. Grade eight, we will be doing math first this morning."

But Janna couldn't concentrate on math. She cupped her chin in her hands and stared at the only decoration on the wall: two maps, one of Canada and the other of the world. Her mind was on Edmonton. If Mr. Groot could walk to Edmonton, so could she. Somehow she'd have to find her way. She couldn't stay here for the rest of her life. In the background the teacher's voice droned on, Sara's pen scratched against her paper, and bare feet shuffled on the wooden floor. Janna turned to Sara. "Do you have a map of

Alberta?" she whispered.

"Is there a problem I can help you with?" The teacher narrowed his eyes and tapped his pencil on Janna's desk as he spoke.

"Uh no, I was just thinking." Janna hastily dipped a spiky looking pen that Sara had given her into the inkwell on the corner of the desk.

"I'd like to see that thought translated into action," the teacher remarked as Janna hastily scanned the book in front of her.

The math wasn't hard but when she tried to write, the pen made spidery scratches across the page and when she pressed harder, it made holes in her paper, oozed ink and blotted out the figures she had just written. She frowned, scratched out her calculations and started again.

By the time the teacher returned to her desk, she had made little progress. "I can't make out what you've written," he said as he leaned over and examined her work. "Weren't you taught penmanship in your last school? Your figures are as poorly formed as a beginner's."

"It's the pen," Janna muttered.

The teacher inspected the pen. "There's nothing wrong with this pen. I suggest that unless you wish to return to the junior grades, you do better than this. Redo this work, please. At recess if necessary."

By noon the school room had become hot and bullflies buzzed relentlessly against the window, but Janna had almost mastered the messy pen. When Mr. Ashley inspected the results of her labours, he merely grunted and walked out.

"What does he expect?" Janna muttered to Sara as she emerged from the sweltering schoolhouse.

"Ssh," Sara whispered. "He's right behind us. He's coming to organize the baseball. The boys have quite a good team," she went on, "except that they usually lose."

"All right!" the teacher shouted from behind them. "Let's play. This time we're going to win!"

"We're playing against the boys from the Dutch church in Edmonton," Sara said.

"Edmonton?" Janna stiffened.

"Yes. We've challenged them to a game after the July picnic."

"Can we go and watch?" Janna asked.

It seemed like an eternity before Sara answered. "Of course," she said. "We're all going."

Chapter Eight

"Janna!" Sara nudged her. "You're day-dreaming again."

"What?" Janna crashed back into the stuffy heat of the crowded classroom. She had been imagining what it would be like when she got back to her family. In her mind, she had just had a shower and a slice of chocolate cheesecake and she was sitting with her mother and Roddy telling them about what had happened.

Sara pointed at the large clock which hung on the wall above the blackboard. "Look. It's three-thirty. School's over. Let's go and buy your scribbler."

Janna sighed and let go of her dream. It would be six weeks before she saw it fulfilled if she waited for the baseball match. Still, she didn't have much choice.

They left the classroom and drifted across the dirt road towards the Neerlandia Co-operative Association swinging their lunch pails in the bright sunshine. The Co-op was a small building with barrels and boxes stacked on the porch outside the door and a gas pump in the yard outside. The clerk was deep in conversation with a customer as they walked in.

Sara wandered towards some shelves piled to the ceiling with bolts of coloured fabric. "You get the scribbler. I just want to look over here. Pa says maybe I can have a new dress when we sell the hogs."

Janna couldn't see any scribblers. There was so much crowded onto shelves behind the counters: rakes, shovels, pans, plates and cups, rows of bottles, cans, little brown bags labelled raisins and tea, and sacks of flour and sugar. Behind the cash register were cigarettes and candy. Janna focussed on the ropes of licorice, suckers, jawbreakers, pink and white peppermints, and little chocolate mice. They were labelled one cent each.

The clerk, a motherly woman in a long apron, was still engrossed in conversation. "Five babies," she was saying, shaking her head as she spoke. "Five! And they are all still alive. It's a miracle." She looked up as Janna took a step towards her. "Can I help you?"

The sight of chocolate was too much for Janna. She could almost taste it. "I'll have two of those," she said pointing to the crouching mice.

The clerk raised her eyebrows. "Two! Are you sure?"

Janna nodded. What harm could it do to spend two cents? Everything was so cheap. She shoved the three pennies the clerk handed her in change into her pocket, and took a mouse out of the small brown bag. She licked its head.

Intoxicating thick sweetness melted through her mouth.

"Did you get the scribbler?" Sara asked.

Janna started guiltily and proffered the bag she was holding. "I forgot," she mumbled, rolling the sugar head into her cheek. "I bought us these."

Sara's eyes were circles. "You bought candy! What will your mother say? And what will you tell the teacher if you don't have a scribbler?"

"It's only two cents," Janna said. "I'll think of something to tell Mr. Ashley. Now, do you want the candy or not?"

Sara shook her head, and then changed her mind and plunged her hand into the bag. She gave the mouse a long slow lick. "We'll get into trouble about this."

"For two cents?" Janna didn't believe it. And nothing happened when they got home, nor at school the next day when she explained that she did not have quite enough money to pay for a scribbler. She hoped that she could use that excuse until it was time for the baseball match. "Maybe we should buy more candy," she suggested to Sara, fingering the remaining pennies in her pocket.

"I don't think so," Sara demurred as they waited for Willie. He had kicked a stone all the way to school that morning and was looking for the same one to kick home again. "I still think there will be trouble when your pa finds out."

"He's not going to find out," Janna said.

"You've forgotten what it's like here. Of course he'll find out. Come on, Willie," Sara added impatiently. "I'm not going to wait for you any longer." She grabbed his hand and marched him forward.

Still, she relented at the first puddle they passed and let Willie fill his pail with tadpoles. She even caught a toad to add to his collection. Janna had to carry the lid of his pail so that he could watch the tadpoles as they walked. "You'd better concentrate," Sara warned him as they crossed a patch of muskeg, balancing on the logs that Oom Klaas had placed for them. Willie, who had his face in his pail, lost his balance when he looked up. Janna fished him out of the water.

"Now what will Tante Marie say?" Sara scolded him.

But Mrs. Vriend scarcely noticed Willie. She was ironing as Janna and Sara walked into the kitchen. "Mrs. Groot came to visit," she said.

"Oh." Janna dropped her lunch pail by the door.

"And last evening Mrs. Groot saw Mrs. Prins," Mrs. Vriend went on.

Sara paled. "Oh, oh," she muttered.

Janna didn't understand. "That's nice," she said.

"And," Mrs. Vriend continued, "Mrs. Prins said she saw you at the Co-op."

"I told you," Sara whispered.

"And she asked Mrs. Groot how all of a sudden the Vriends were so rich that Janna Vriend had money to spend on candy."

"I only spent two cents," Janna said. "And you don't have to worry. The teacher said I can use paper at school."

Mrs. Vriend frowned. "If you didn't need the scribbler, why didn't you bring the nickel back home?"

"I'm sorry," Janna said. "But it was only two cents."

"Only two cents," Mr. Vriend barked later when he heard the story. "And where do you think you can get another two cents?"

Janna glowered at him. Even Dennis would make a better father than him.

Mr. Vriend turned away and sank into the chair in front of the wood stove. "Two cents may not be very much," he said more quietly. "But it is more than we have to spare right now. You will have to learn to row with the oars you have been given. You can work to earn that money back."

"Mr. Groen wants someone to wash his curtains," Mrs. Vriend said. "Perhaps he will pay you to do it for him."

Oom Klaas took the pipe from his mouth and looked up from the newspaper he was reading. "Sara can help," he said, meeting his daughter's eyes.

Sara looked down. "We'll stop there on the way home from school tomorrow."

Mr. Groen's house was tiny and smelled of smoke. Janna and Sara waited inside the door beside an axe, various gardening tools, a gun, and a harness hanging on the wall. Meanwhile, Mr. Groen, a bent and crusty old man, puffed at his pipe and took down his dusty curtains from the three rooms in his scantily furnished house.

He handed them to Janna without a word and merely

took another draw from his pipe when she said she would bring them back as soon as she could.

"He's not very friendly," she muttered as she and Sara made their way home. "And the smell of his pipe was awful."

"He smokes sweet clover. He's a bachelor," Sara said. "Pa says he's afraid of women."

"Yuck. Even these curtains smell of smoke and dust. And they're so dirty you can't tell what colour they're supposed to be."

"I think Mrs. Hiemstra made them." Sara attempted to walk along the length of a tree trunk which had fallen beside the path. "They'll go white when we wash them."

"Huh," Janna muttered. "Washing these is going to be worth a lot more than two cents."

They had to get up earlier the next day to begin the washing before school. Sara made a fire in the stove and Janna carried buckets of water from the well. The water was icy cold and slopped against her legs as she walked. After they heated it on the stove, the boiling hot water scalded her hands as she filled the tub. Then Janna battled to crank the hand operated machine while the harsh smell of lye soap stung her nostrils.

"Don't forget you must rinse them one more time," Mrs. Vriend said as she helped them empty the machine and refill it with more buckets of icy water from the well. "You must put blueing in the water."

And after that, they still had to feed the dripping curtains through the wringer. Pockets of water trapped in the fabric where Janna hadn't lined it up correctly, squirted them and by the time the curtains were hanging on the line, both Sara and Janna and the kitchen floor were drenched.

"They'll be dry by the time you get home," Mrs. Vriend said cheerfully. "And you can iron them."

The ironing took almost as long as the washing. The little metal irons had to be heated over the wood stove, and reheated as they grew cool. The curtains were stiff, wrinkled and resilient. Janna had to sprinkle them with water and then press the iron over and over again, doing one small patch at a time, before they smoothed out at all. She burned her fingers testing the iron, and the smell of burned flesh, wood stove, steam and hot cotton made her feel ill, but eventually the curtains were ironed, and they looked white and fresh. Sara folded them carefully and put them in a large brown paper bag to take to Mr. Groen after school the next day.

"I hope he appreciates how much work that was," Janna said as they left for school. "We should have told him it would be ten dollars."

Sara giggled. "I just hope he gives us something."

Mr. Groen took the bag Janna proffered without looking inside. "Thank you," he muttered. For a moment, Janna thought he was going to close the door on them, but he held up his hand and disappeared inside.

"He's gone to get the money," she whispered to Sara.

Mr. Groen reappeared at the door and shoved something into Janna's hand. "That is for you. For your help." And then he retreated into his house, shutting the door behind him.

Janna stood dumbfounded. In her hand were two empty cotton sugar sacks.

"He can't be serious," she blurted to Sara. "Look what he gave me for doing all that work!" She threw the sugar sacks down on the ground in disgust. "What does he think I'm going to do with those?"

"Don't throw them away." Sara picked up the sacks. "You can use them. My mother always made runners for the table from sugar sacks. She embroidered them."

"I can't do embroidery," Janna snapped. "And I don't need table runners. What I need is two cents to get Mr... I mean Pa off my back." She stepped aside to let a woman who was coming up the path towards Mr. Groen's house go past.

"Good afternoon Sara and Janna," the woman said. There was a delicious odour of bread coming from the covered basket she held. "Have you been visiting Mr. Groen?"

"We washed his curtains for him," Sara said.

"And he gave me these." Janna snatched the sugar sacks from Sara'a hand and flourished them angrily.

The woman stopped. "I was looking for some fabric," she said. "If you don't want them..."

"Janna needs a scribbler," Sara said. "She was hoping that Mr. Groen would give her two cents."

"I don't have any money," the woman said. She paused and cocked her head. "But I think I do have a scribbler. My boy didn't go back to school this year and I think his scribbler still has pages in it. Wait for me, girls, and we will go and look as soon as I have given this bread to poor old Mr. Groen."

And so one problem was solved, and only the problem of waiting five long weeks before she could get back to Edmonton remained. But the days did pass and Janna almost got used to the routine of waking up at five in the mornings and finding and milking the cows before she and Sara went to school. And she almost got used to all the other chores: fetching firewood, feeding the pigs, weeding the garden, helping with the washing and the cleaning, and getting water. She almost got used to the outhouse and the Eaton's catalogue toilet paper, and the Saturday night bath, and Sunday in church.

But still, even though Mrs. Vriend was always kind and she grew to love her and Sara and Oom Klaas, Janna longed to go home, especially when she caught glimpses of Oom Klaas with his arm around Sara's shoulder, or saw Willie sitting tight against Sara as she read to him. From so far away the idea of Dennis living with them didn't seem so bad.

However, on the long walks to and from the little white schoolhouse through brilliant pink fireweed and violet columbine, her homesickness faded to a dull ache, and while they were paddling in the stony creek on days when the sun was hot overhead, or building forts for Willie in the brush piles that Oom Klaas and Mr. Vriend cleared from the land, she was almost happy. Only at night, when she lay in the bed with Sara, loneliness uncurled itself from its lair where it hid during the days, and she wondered whether her mother and Dennis were already married and she wished that she had been the maid of honour, and she counted the days until the picnic and the baseball match when she could get back to Edmonton.

In June the boys began to practise in earnest. At recess they set poles into the ground and practised high jump and broad jump for the competitions which took place during the picnic, and after school, the baseball practices became more intense. But inside the classroom the days still dragged and the room grew hotter and hotter and the bullflies buzzed more lazily around the window.

One recess Piet caught a row of somnolent bullflies and threaded them onto a stiff bristle he had pulled from the broom in the cloakroom. "Look at this!" he exclaimed, brandishing the line of frantically buzzing flies. He held it over his head and then let go. The bristle hovered in the air, diving erratically up and down.

"Let's all make one," Jakob suggested, "and we can race."

But the teacher shook his head. "There will be no cruelty in this classroom," he said. "Not even to flies."

There was a muffled chorus of protest.

"I've got something much more interesting than dirty old bullflies," one of the girls whispered.

"What?" Janna was curious.

Marta indicated the lunch box she was carrying. "Come behind the willows and I'll show you."

Janna and Sara and several other girls followed her to the trees. "What is it?" Sara asked.

Marta peered around the bushes. "Where's Mr. Ashley?"

"He's over by the broad jump talking to Jakob," Janna replied. "Show us what you've got."

"All right." Marta opened the lid of her lunch box. "Look." She held up a small package. "I sent for a free sample from Ponds."

"But what is it?" Janna asked as the girls crowded in to get a better look at Marta's package.

"It's face powder," Sara said. "Open it, Marta, so we can smell it."

"Face powder!" Janna said. "Who wants face powder?"

The girls ignored her. "I was going to wear some to school this morning, but then I didn't dare," Marta said, as she opened the sample.

"Why not?" Janna asked. "What's the big deal about face powder?"

"If you think you're so clever, you put some on," Sara said.

"Sure." Janna held out her hand for the cotton wad that

came with the sample, and then dabbed it liberally over her face. "There," she said. "So what's the problem?"

The problem was that the teacher told Mr. and Mrs. Vriend that Janna had been wearing make-up to school. As a result, she had to do extra chores for the rest of the week.

"But it was only face powder," she had protested. "At home..." But she bit back her words. There was no point in making a fuss. She would be at home in a little under two weeks. In two weeks' time she would see Roddy and her mother.

And then it was one week, and then four days, and three days. And then it was Friday and the picnic was the next day.

It was still dark when Janna woke on Saturday morning. Finally! The day had come! She lay for a moment listening to the wind whistling at the window. She shivered as she got up and looked outside. The sky was grey and thick with swirling clouds, and the trees swayed and bent in the wind. In the distance thunder rolled.

Chapter Nine

It was drizzling by the time Janna and Sara had found the cows and milked them. Janna's damp hair stuck to her face, and her skirt, wet from the grass, slapped against her legs as she walked.

"I think the baseball game will be cancelled," Mr. Vriend said after he read the Bible passage at breakfast.

Janna's stomach clenched. "Perhaps it's not raining in Edmonton, or perhaps it will clear up."

"Perhaps," Mr. Vriend agreed as he spread his thick soft pancake with butter.

Janna stared out the window at the black sky. How could this happen today of all days? If the game were cancelled she didn't think she would survive. She closed her eyes and imagined Roddy's face, but his image wavered and flickered in her mind and finally turned into Willie's face. Janna brushed away a tear with the back of her hand.

"Don't get so upset," Mrs. Vriend said putting her arm around Janna's shoulders. "We need this rain and if we can't have the picnic today, we will hold it next week."

"Really?" Janna felt cheered. "You mean we'll go to Edmonton for the baseball next week?"

Mrs. Vriend ruffled her hair. "Or maybe we'll hold it here."

Janna's hope died. "I was looking forward to going into Edmonton."

"Well, I'm on my way to the Co-op to pick up some supplies," Mr. Vriend said. "I'll find out what's happening when I get there." He jammed his hat on his head and opened the kitchen door. A gust of wind spattered raindrops across the kitchen floor. "I won't be long."

Mrs. Vriend lit the coal oil lamp and settled at the kitchen table with her sewing. "Tell us a story, Tante, while we wait for the picnic," Willie said, snuggling up to her.

"Yes, yes," the others chorused, crowding around.

Mrs. Vriend put down her sewing. "All right. It is a holiday, even if the picnic is cancelled. Did I ever tell you about the time..."

Janna wasn't listening. She stood by the cold window staring out at the clouds scudding across the sky and the rain lashing the trees.

"The game is off," Mr. Vriend said when he finally burst through the door together with a blast of wind and rain. "It's raining in Edmonton too so there'll be no picnic today, but..." he added holding up his hand to silence the groan from the children, "we will hold it as soon as the weather clears up."

"And the baseball?"

"The Edmonton boys will come here next Saturday."

Janna felt her world collapse.

"I picked up the mail," Mr. Vriend went on as a muddy puddle formed at his feet. He flourished a sheaf of letters and held one out to his wife. "News from Holland. And here's one for you, Klaas. From the government."

Mrs. Vriend grabbed her letter and ripped it open, but Oom Klaas frowned. "Nothing from the government is good news," he said.

"That's not surprising. I heard this morning that Premier Brownlea is in trouble. Apparently a young lady and her father are suing him for damages." Mr. Vriend raised his eyebrows and glanced at the children. "But I will tell you about that later. The paper also said the relief strike may spread to all of Alberta." He held out an envelope to Janna as he spoke. "And here's a letter for you."

"What?" Janna felt as though she was struggling to the surface from deep underwater.

"Your mother says that everything is fine at home," Mrs. Vriend said, scanning the pages from Holland. "And that Anna will get married in the fall."

"Good," Mr. Vriend said. "That's good."

"Are you listening?" Mrs. Vriend asked. "I said your sister is getting married." There were tears in her eyes. "I wish we could go to the wedding."

"Who is your letter from, Janna?" Sara asked.

Janna stared at the envelope in her hands. "I don't know."

"Sometimes I am afraid that we will never see any of them again," Mrs. Vriend said, wiping her eyes with her apron.

"Open it," Sara commanded. "And tell me who it's from."

It was from Charles:

Dear Janna,

Thank you for your letter. I have looked for your locket, but I did not find it. You are welcome to look again yourself when you return. Your adventure with sinking cows sounded fun. Nothing here is interesting, especially school. My grandma says that she still misses your mother. She has tried two other people but they were not as reliable. Now she has no one to help her and she is very miffed.

"Read this," Oom Klaas said, handing his letter to Mr. Vriend before Janna could respond to Sara's demand. He sank into a chair by the table and dropped his head into his hands. "I hoped they'd wait until after the harvest, when I could work on the roads."

"What are you talking about?" Mrs. Vriend looked anxious.

"I didn't pay the land tax on the farm last year or the year before," Oom Klaas answered. "I couldn't. I didn't have it." He passed his hand through his hair. "But the government wants the money now, or I will lose the place."

There was a hushed silence in the room. "Do you mean we'd have to leave Neerlandia?" Sara whispered finally.

Oom Klaas nodded.

"It won't come to that," Mr. Vriend said. "There must be something we can do."

"I thought I could pay off some of what I owe by working on the roads."

"Good. So do it. As soon as the harvest..."

"That is the problem," Oom Klaas interrupted, looking up. "I can't wait till the fall. I have to work now, or pay now. They will not wait. And how can I leave the farm? You don't have the experience to manage the farm alone, Simon."

There was another long silence. Even Willie sat still on Mrs. Vriend's lap.

"We will get a new loan for some of the debt," Mr. Vriend said, breaking the silence. "I read in the paper that Ottawa is passing a new bill to help farmers. The article said it would save them millions in interest, and I will go back to Edmonton and get a job — perhaps the brickyard is hiring again — and help you with the payments. And then, in the fall after the harvest, you can work on the roads to repay the rest."

Mrs. Vriend put her arms around Oom Klaas' shoulders. "I will also go to Edmonton and look for a job."

"No, Marie." Mr. Vriend's voice was adamant. "You will stay here with the children and help Klaas until fall."

It took a moment for Janna to grasp the significance of

what was being said: Mr. Vriend was going back to Edmonton. She crushed the letter she was holding into a tight ball in her fist. How could she make Mr. Vriend take her with him? And then it came to her. She opened her fingers and smoothed out the letter.

"I could come with you, Pa," she said. "And I could work too for the rest of the summer. I could work for Mrs. Randolph." She held up the letter. "Charles said she is looking for someone." Janna held her breath as she waited for a reply.

Mrs. Vriend looked as though she were going to protest. Her eyes met Janna's and then she smiled. "I think that is a good idea, Simon," she said to Mr. Vriend. "Janna could take care of you. She is almost fifteen now. It will be good for her to work."

Janna reached out and took Mrs. Vriend's hand. "You mean I can go?" she asked. "To Edmonton?" For the first time it occurred to her that when she got home she would miss Mrs. Vriend.

"I think your mother is right," Mr. Vriend said. "We will write to Mrs. Randolph immediately and ask if you can work for her."

The following days passed in a blur. The picnic was a haze of sunshine, ice cream, lemonade, the three-legged race, the sack race and wheelbarrow race. But Janna's main preoccupation was waiting for a reply from Mrs. Randolph.

And after Mrs. Randolph wrote to say that she would hire Janna, there was another flurry of preparations before

Janna and Mr. Vriend squeezed in the cab of Mr. Fisher's truck and travelled back to Edmonton with the cream cans rattling and bumping in the back.

Chapter Ten

By the time they reached the city, the trees along the streets of Edmonton cast slanting shadows across the pavement. Janna pressed her face against the truck window and stared at the sidewalks, stores and street-lamps. The warm glow of light helped soothe the ache she felt at leaving Mrs. Vriend and Sara.

They stopped at a small four-roomed house down a muddy track at the bottom of a hill. The house was dark inside and smelled of mould and wood smoke. Mr. Vriend lit a coal oil lamp. "Looks just the same as when we left," he said with a grimace, glancing around at the cracked linoleum floor and bare walls. "We can get our furniture from the neighbours tomorrow, but for tonight we'll have to make do."

Janna put down the box she had carried in from the street. "I should start work tomorrow. Mrs. Randolph said she wants me as soon as possible."

Mr. Vriend shrugged. "Mrs. Randolph can wait one more

day. We'll have to get settled first. Apart from getting our furniture, we need to buy groceries and get some wood for the stove, and I am sure in the light of day we will find that this place needs cleaning. But first we must have water. I'll go to the pump now and fill a bucket."

Janna stood for a long time at the window after he had gone. It was starting to rain. She stared at the misty lights from house windows up the hill. Somewhere in the city was Charles' house. She closed her eyes and tried to imagine the painting on the study wall, but the image wouldn't come. She quelled a stab of anxiety and reminded herself that by the following night she would be back with her family, with her mother, Roddy, Omie — and Dennis. She dreamed of them when she went to sleep that night, curled on a blanket on the hard wooden floor. In her dream her mother had forgotten her. She awoke the next morning feeling stiff and sore.

"We still have sandwiches left from yesterday," Mr. Vriend said, when he met her in the kitchen. He passed her a thick slab of bread and lard. "And Mrs. Tassie from next door has made some coffee. She says we can get our goods from her basement as soon as we are ready."

"I'm ready." Janna jumped to her feet. The quicker everything got organized, the quicker she could go to Mrs. Randolph.

Mr. Vriend and two neighbours carried the table and chairs, and a rough wooden bed. They struggled with a large black sideboard with shelves and a mirror. "Ugly thing," Mr. Vriend muttered. "But don't tell your mother I said so."

There was a rocking chair and a wardrobe and a sagging chesterfield with a worn patchwork cover. Janna carried boxes of saucepans, linen and plates. By lunch time everything was moved and Janna and Mrs. Tassie had scrubbed the floors and wiped dust from the windows.

"Can I go and see Mrs. Randolph now?" Janna asked as soon as she had greedily gulped the potato soup that the cheerful Mrs. Tassie brought over.

"Tomorrow will be soon enough," Mr. Vriend said. "We still have a lot to do around here."

Janna forced herself to be patient. If she tried to escape, perhaps Mr. Vriend would come looking for her. She couldn't risk anything going wrong. So she scrambled along the shrubby bank of the North Saskatchewan River collecting driftwood in the trembling shade of aspens and poplars while birds chirped and the water splashed against the banks. A group of boys were standing ankle deep in the water, fishing. Janna stared at them and thought of her father. He loved fishing. Her thoughts drifted to her mother. She wondered whether she was still living with Omie or whether she and Dennis had found somewhere else to live. And she thought about Roddy and remembered the soft feel of him when he crawled into bed with her in the mornings. She ached to get home.

But first she had to struggle back to the house with an armload of river-smooth sticks. "You better clean out the stove and fill the buckets from the pump," Mr. Vriend said as she dumped her bundle on the woodpile beside the outhouse. "After that we should go to Ebbers to get some sugar and tea and coffee. I hope they will open our account again."

Janna gritted her teeth as she began to scour the stove and reminded herself that she wouldn't have to carry wood ever again, or water. She wouldn't have to clean out dirty wood stoves or use an outhouse or bathe in a metal tub in the kitchen. Nor would she have to walk everywhere, she thought later as she and Mr. Vriend made their way down a wooden sidewalk above a potholed gravel track towards the grocery store. Her mother would drive her in the car.

"There's Joe Olthuis," Mr. Vriend said as they approached the corner. He waved to a man standing outside the grocery store.

The man returned Mr. Vriend's greeting. "So you're back? How are things with Klaas in Neerlandia?"

"Crops are looking good," Mr. Vriend replied. "Much of it is in shot blade. Should start to head soon. But there's a problem about taxes. That's why I'm back. I need work."

"These are tough times," Mr. Olthuis said, nodding his head gravely.

"We need some changes," Mr. Vriend said. "We need a new government with some new ideas for one thing. And that Premier Brownlea . . ." He glanced at Janna and handed her a scrap of paper. "You go and give the list to Mrs. Olthuis," he said, "while I go round back for the coal oil."

"I read the Premier brought that girl from Edson when she was only eighteen," Janna heard him say as she walked through the door past neat pyramids of cans displayed in the window and gave the list to the lady behind the counter.

"So you're back, Janna," Mrs. Olthuis said as she took the scrap of paper on which Mr. Vriend had scrawled the grocery list. "How is your mother?"

"Fine," Janna said.

"I heard you're going to work for the old English lady," Mrs. Olthuis went on. "Well, I wish you luck. Your mother was a saint to put up with her for so long." She poured some tea leaves into the basket of the scale on the counter. "But you'll be all right. You're young and strong. Just don't let old Mrs.... now what was her name?"

"Mrs. Randolph," Janna replied.

"That's it," Mrs. Olthuis said as she pushed the bags across the counter to Janna. "Just don't let Mrs. Randolph bother you."

Janna reminded herself of that advice the next morning. "Staff use the back entrance," Mrs. Randolph said when she opened the door to Janna's knock. She closed the door again in Janna's face.

Stay calm, Janna told herself as she made her way round to the back door and knocked again. In a little while it will all be over.

Mrs. Randolph led Janna into the kitchen. "Today I will supervise and make sure you know exactly what I expect you to do." She pointed at the white porcelain sink. "You can start with the breakfast dishes. Now when you run the water do not use hot water excessively. Electricity is an expensive commodity. And do not waste soap."

"Come along now," she went on as Janna stared round the kitchen. "I won't tolerate any dawdling. I had to let the last girl go because she was a slacker. I intend to find out today what kind of worker you are."

"Stay calm," Janna muttered under her breath as she turned on the brass taps above the sink.

"Now on Mondays, of course," Mrs. Randolph went on, "you will do the washing, and on Tuesdays, you will do the ironing. The rest of the week, please do the usual house-cleaning. Sweep and wash the linoleum. Buff the wood floors. And dust of course." She stopped speaking and picked up one of the plates Janna had just washed. She held it up to the light from the window and then dropped it back into the water. "There's a speck on that plate. Now, on Thursdays I would like the silver polished. And on Fridays, you can scour the bathroom."

Stay calm, Janna repeated again as she stared down into the sink and clenched her teeth to stop herself from attacking Mrs. Randolph with a dish rag.

"Now if you're finished with the dishes, you can start upstairs. Bring the broom and a brush and pan."

The study door was closed as Mrs. Randolph led Janna down the passage towards the stairs. Janna looked at it longingly. She was tempted to fling herself through the door, but she resisted the urge. If she did anything like that Mrs. Randolph would probably fire her and drag her out before she'd had a chance even to look at the painting.

"You may start in Charles' room," Mrs. Randolph said, indicating one of the doors which opened onto the landing at the top of the stairs. "Dust carefully and don't break anything."

Janna remembered Charles' wide smile and bright eyes as she flicked her feather duster over a book of stamps open on the dresser, a glass case with butterflies on pins, model airplanes hanging from the ceiling and a bookcase stacked with thick hardcover books: *Tom Brown's Schooldays, Tom Sawyer, Just William.*

Mrs. Randolph appeared at the door. "I hope you swept under the bed." She ran her finger over the surface of the dresser and the chest of drawers. "Your mother was a very good housekeeper," was all she said. "Now go ahead and do my son's room. Don't disturb any of his papers. He is most particular about that."

Janna had still not had an opportunity to escape Mrs. Randolph's scrutiny when she heard Charles burst through the door. Mrs. Randolph, who was hovering by the bathroom door watching Janna scour the bath with scratchy steel wool and abrasive powder, turned and called to him, "Is that you, Charles?"

Janna rinsed the powder off her hands and straightened her back. Perhaps now finally, Mrs. Randolph would leave her alone long enough for her to get to the study.

"Hi," Charles replied, bounding up the stairs.

"Don't run like that," Mrs. Randolph said. "I've told you and I've told you again that it's dangerous. You might fall and hurt yourself."

Charles' steps slowed.

"Where have you been?" Mrs. Randolph asked. "I expected you home sooner."

"I told you I was going to a matinee with Norman at the Princess."

"I wish you wouldn't spend so much time with Norman. You know I don't think he is a suitable companion."

Charles continued as though she hadn't spoken. "We saw George Arliss in *The House of Rothschild.* It was swell. A man..."

"You know his mother used to be in service, and there was a rumour that his father..." Mrs. Randolph went on. She stopped when Janna appeared at the door. "Yes?"

Janna felt awkward. "I've finished the bathroom," she said, holding the scouring pad behind her back.

"You came!" Charles exclaimed. "I hoped you would. Have you rescued any more sinking cows?"

Janna smiled. "Oh sure. I found two in your front yard on my way here."

Charles grinned. "Well that explains why the neighbours are always complaining that their cows keep disappearing."

"You may go now, Janna," Mrs. Randolph said, frowning.

"But I haven't finished downstairs," Janna protested. "I haven't dusted in the study."

"You can do that tomorrow," Mrs. Randolph replied.

Tomorrow! No, Janna couldn't wait another day. She shook her head. "I must do it now," she said. "I don't like leaving a job half done."

Mrs. Randolph nodded. "I suppose you are right."

"I'll help," Charles said, following Janna down the stairs.

Mrs. Randolph compressed her lips. "Charles, I think you should go and practise your piano. Janna is being paid to work. I will show her what needs to be done."

Janna ignored Mrs. Randolph's peevish tone. Finally! Finally, she was going to get back to the painting. This time, nothing could go wrong. No one would stop her from staring at the painting as she dusted it, and then the lady would reach out to her and softly, softly, she would swim through time to where she belonged.

Janna heard the clear ringing notes of the piano as Mrs. Randolph opened the study door. "Don't move anything on the desk," she said.

Trembling, Janna turned her eyes to the wall above the fireplace. To the painting. But there was no painting. It was gone. The wall was bare. Frantically she spun around. The painting was not in the study.

Janna struggled to speak though her lips had dried and her tongue stuck to the roof of her mouth. "Didn't there used to be a painting hanging on that wall above the fireplace?"

Mrs. Randolph frowned. "Yes," she said. "My son has sent it to Toronto to be cleaned. Now, I suggest you begin dusting the bookshelves. Make sure that you dust the tops of the books."

Chapter Eleven

Janna left the house in a daze. Stately pink peonies, rosebushes, and periwinkle blue delphiniums blurred as she stumbled down the path.

"Janna! Wait!" Charles' feet clattered against the sidewalk as he ran to catch up.

She wiped her eyes with the back of her hand. "What?"

"I just wanted to make sure..." Charles shrugged and then grinned. "Well, I thought I'd check you hadn't run into any more cows."

Janna smiled faintly, "I told you. I already rescued them all."

Charles kicked a pebble down the sidewalk. "I'm sorry about my grandma. My father says she's snobbish because she's had so many disappointments. I hope she didn't offend you."

"I was thinking about something else," Janna replied with a shrug.

Charles scuffed at a crack in the concrete. "I wanted you

to know that I'm not like that."

"I didn't think you were."

"I just thought you seemed upset when you left." Charles followed Janna as she stepped down from the raised walk and dodged across the main road through the cyclists and chunky cars.

"No. By the way, when do you get the painting back, the one that hangs above the fireplace in the study?"

"Do you like it? I think it's gone until spring. My father's cousin is going to bring it and he only comes once a year."

"Spring! That's almost a year away!"

"Not long enough for my grandma." Charles grinned and lowered his voice. "She hates that picture because, although he was already engaged to her, my grandfather got it from a Boer girl he fell in love with when he was fighting for the English in the Boer War."

"What happened?"

"One day when my grandfather went to see the girl, he found the English had burned her house down and taken her to an internment camp. The painting was hanging on the only wall that was still standing. He took the painting but when he went to the camp to find her, the girl had died. My grandfather said he could sometimes see her behind the leaves in the picture."

"I saw her too," Janna burst out. "I know this sounds a little crazy, but my grandmother has that painting now, I mean in the future, and I saw it on her wall, and then one night, as I was staring at it, a lady came out from behind the bush and suddenly I was falling and I landed in your father's library. In the past and..." Her rush of words dried up when she saw Charles' grin.

"Good imagination!"

"But it's true," Janna cried. "I can prove it. I know what's going to happen in the future." She wished again that she had paid more attention to social studies as her mind cast about for something she could tell him. "For one thing, there's going to be a second world war," she said. "It starts in...uh...1930-something. 1938 or 1939, I think."

"My father says that too," Charles answered. "It was in the paper last week that Germany is threatening to stop trading with Britain and France. My father says that's only the beginning. He says Hitler..."

"Hitler was a terrible man. He introduced concentration camps and killed over 6 million Jews. But the Allies won in the end, after they dropped the atom bombs on Japan."

Charles stared at her curiously. "You're making all that up," he said.

A wave of despair flooded over Janna. She had no idea how to convince him, or how to get home without the painting. And so the days passed slowly in an endless fog of drudgery and tedium. She got up each morning before the sun was up, lit the stove, filled the buckets at the pump and then prepared the morning meal for Mr. Vriend. After that, she climbed the long steps up the hill and trudged through the city and across the bridge to the Randolphs. There she scrubbed and scoured and scraped, until bleach, soap, abrasive powder and ammonia scalded her skin and scorched her nose and lungs. Her hands turned red, dried out and cracked, and the smell of cleaners seemed to cling to her clothes and her hair so that wherever she went, the aroma of ammonia and bleach followed. She longed to shower when she got home, but at her home there was no gush of hot water as there was at Charles' house. Instead, Mr. Vriend filled an iron tub for her every Saturday evening, just as he had on the farm in Neerlandia.

The only good thing about the daily toil at the Randolphs was that at the end of it, Charles usually walked part of the way home with her, and Janna looked forward the whole lonely day to his company. He was the only friend she had, the only person with whom she could laugh and make jokes. When he came home from school, he always came to talk to her despite his grandmother's admonitions about homework and piano practice. Sometimes they walked along staring into store windows, making fun of the stuffy store clerks who glared at them. Sometimes Charles had money and they bought striped sticks of candy which, when sucked slowly, lasted Janna for the whole walk home, or bulls-eyes which melted slowly layer upon coloured layer, like the rings of Saturn, until they finally dissolved into beads of anisette. Sometimes they talked about things that had happened at school: how Charles and Norm skipped school and went skinny dipping in the creek, and how they had stolen the detention book from the principal's office so that no one had detention that day. And Jana told how she and a friend had taken a formaldehyde frog from science class and put it into their rival's stew in home economics.

Mrs. Randolph, however, scowled if she saw them together. "Your grandma thinks I'm an unsuitable companion, doesn't she?" Janna remarked one day when Charles caught up with her, out of breath, several blocks from his house.

Charles grinned. "I don't know," he said. "I've never asked her."

"Then why do you always leave your house after me? Or before?"

Charles grimaced. "It just seems easier. My grandma thinks everyone I know is unsuitable. I'm not supposed to see Norm or Geoff this week because Geoff's sister saw us smoking in the ravine last week and my grandma got to hear about it."

"You don't smoke, do you?" Janna asked. "Don't you know you'll get lung cancer?"

"I never heard that before. Everyone smokes in the ravine and no one I know has got lung cancer." He stopped walking and pointed to a new poster advertising a forthcoming attraction at the Princess. "Look at that. I bet it's really good. Maybe we should go sometime, you and I." He blushed as he spoke and turned back to the poster. "I mean just sometime."

Janna's heart quickened. Was he asking her out? Like a date? She stared at her shoes. "Sure," she said. "Maybe. Sometime."

Neither of them spoke for a few minutes. Janna glanced at Charles out of the corner of her eye and her heart quickened again. It was hard to describe, even to herself how she felt. For a little while she had known that she liked him. She thought about him as she dusted, buffed the floor, changed sheets and swept. And if he was in the house, his presence was almost like a tingling in her skin. And on those evenings when he didn't walk some of the way home with her, her feet felt like lead, and the road stretched ahead interminably.

"My grandma won't be home for supper tonight," Charles remarked, as they approached the High Level Bridge where he usually turned back. "She left the house just after you did, so I don't have to be home. I might as well walk all the way with you."

Janna grinned. "Do you think you should? It's still quite a long way. I bet your grandma wouldn't want you to tire out your little tootsies."

"My little tootsies can walk just as far as your little tootsies," Charles said. He broke into a run. "And a lot faster." They raced across the bridge high above the water, flame-tipped in the light of the late afternoon sun.

"All right," Charles said, slowing down when they

reached the other side. "Now which way?"

"Jasper, and down the hill to 101," Janna said, pausing to catch her breath.

They crossed at an intersection where a policeman in white gloves stood in the middle of the road on a raised stool and directed the traffic with hand signals. At the next intersection, they plunged recklessly through honking cars and swerving bicycles.

"What's that?" Charles asked when they finally reached the steps that led down the hill. He pointed at a large patch of cultivated green in the distance.

"Everyone calls it the Chinaman's garden," Janna said as they started down the steps. "Pa says they grow the best vegetables in town. They sell them at the market on Saturday mornings."

"It'd be a swell place to raid," Charles said.

"What do you mean?" Janna nodded to a man and woman whom she passed every evening.

"I mean to raid, you know, to get vegetables. Haven't you ever been on a raid?"

Janna shook her head.

Charles rolled his eyes. "I suppose that's because you're a girl."

"Of course it's not," Janna snapped. "Where I come from, girls can do anything boys can do. It's just that nobody raids vegetable gardens anymore."

"I suppose you're right," Charles agreed. "Now that we

are just about fifteen, we are too old for that sort of thing." He grinned at Janna. "But I bet you're too much of a scaredy cat to go on a raid anyway."

"I am not a scaredy cat," Janna retorted. "What would I want to go on a raid for? Our neighbours are always bringing us vegetables."

"Nothing tastes quite like the vegetables you get in a raid," Charles said as they reached the bottom of the steps and turned along the rutted track to Janna's house. "When we were young, Norm and I used to raid all the neighbours' gardens until Norm's mother found out. She nearly had kittens; she thought we'd get arrested, but Norm calmed her down and persuaded her not to tell my grandma." Charles looked in the direction of the large market garden. "It'd be quite fun to go on a raid again. Specially from a big garden like that. Pity you're such a fraidy cat."

"I don't see what's so exciting about stealing a bunch of vegetables," Janna retorted.

"Stealing!" Charles exclaimed indignantly. "It's not *stealing*. It's raiding, which is quite different. Come on. Let's just walk past the garden and have a look at it." The fenced garden was covered in neat rows of flourishing foliage: ruby-tinted beets, blue-green cabbages, lacy carrot ferns, and climbing beans and peas. "They have everything," he said, peering through the strands of barbed wire. "And look — radishes. I love radishes."

"There's a gardener over there," Janna said, indicating a

man who had risen from behind a row of peas.

Charles backed away from the fence. "Usually one goes on raids at night; this would be a challenge."

"There's another gardener," Janna said.

"That needn't be a problem. We could stage a diversion." Charles grinned.

"And another," Janna said as another figure rose into view.

"Perhaps we could set a fence post on fire and then when they all came to investigate..."

Janna shook her head. "Or we could wait ten minutes." She pointed at the gardeners who had picked up their tools and were walking away. "It looks as though they are packing up, or having a break perhaps."

"You're a genius," Charles conceded. "So? Are you coming?"

Janna grimaced. "I think you're mad," she said. "But anything you can do, I can do better."

"All right! Let's see who gets the most booty. But if anything goes wrong — separate. Where could we meet?"

"The brickyard," Janna said, pointing to a building close to the river.

The garden was deserted as they lifted the wire and crawled underneath. "Just wait until you taste those radishes," Charles whispered. "You'll thank me for this."

"Maybe not," Janna muttered as she unhooked her dress from the spikes on the wire. She paused, listening, but there was only the faint hum of traffic from up the hill, and in the distance, the shrill whistle of a factory siren.

"Come on," Charles said, slithering forward on his stomach. "Let's get radishes first."

"You sound like Peter Rabbit." Janna was too tense to go farther than the first row they reached: pale green, tender, young lettuces. She plucked a leaf and nibbled at the edge. It did taste delicious, perhaps because she was hungry. Janna picked another leaf.

Charles slithered towards the radishes. He glanced around when he reached them and then raised himself to his knees and began to pull out handfuls of round red globes from the soft black earth. "Look at these," he whispered as he brushed off the soil. "They're perfect. I told you this was a good idea."

He spoke too soon. "Hey!" a gardener brandishing a trowel shouted in an unfriendly tone. Janna flattened her rigid body against the ground.

Charles' face froze in an expression of horror as the man hopped over the rows towards him. Then he burst into action and fled towards the fence with the man in close pursuit.

Janna didn't move as feet pounded past her. She waited until the shouting faded into the distance and then she cautiously raised her head. Both figures were disappearing around the corner. Surprised to find that fear hadn't paralyzed her completely, Janna crawled back to the fence, collecting Charles' scattered radishes as she went.

She shoved them in her pocket, eased out under the fence and brushed off the dust from her dress. Trying to breathe evenly and to look as nonchalant as possible, she strolled in the direction of the brickyard.

She found Charles, pale and out of breath, crouched behind a pile of bricks. "Thank goodness it's you," he said when he saw her. "Did you see that weapon the gardener was waving? I thought I was a goner." He collapsed against the bricks. "You were right. We're too old for this kind of thing."

Janna sank down beside him and pulled a radish out of her pocket. "Here," she said as she passed it to him. "Have a radish. Nothing tastes as good as vegetables you get from a raid."

Charles burst out laughing. "I like you Janna Vriend," he said as he took the radish. "I like you a lot."

Chapter Twelve

Charles' words echoed through Janna's mind as she stoked and lit the old wood stove, and as she peeled potatoes, carrots and turnips. *I like you, Janna.* She wondered whether he liked her as much as she liked him.

Mr. Vriend arrived home to the warm smell of vegetable stew an hour later. He looked tired; his face was drawn and his shoulders drooped as he walked in the door.

"Supper is ready," Janna said, laying the plates on the table.

"Thank you." Mr. Vriend collapsed into a chair and pulled off his shabby shoes. He rested his hands in his head. "I found nothing again today," he said eventually.

Janna looked at him in surprise. He didn't usually talk much, especially about himself.

"I walked and I walked and I walked," Mr. Vriend went on. "I went into every business on the street. I knocked on every door. And on every street corner I saw the others, hopeless, holding their newspapers, going in the opposite direction. But nothing, nothing, nothing. Not for them, not for me."

Janna noticed there was blood on his socks. She felt unexpectedly sympathetic. "The Depression will end. I know it will." She remembered, although she didn't say, that it ended with a war.

Mr. Vriend stared at the window. "I don't know what to do. Sometimes I even ask myself if it was a mistake to come to this new country."

"I wouldn't want to be anywhere else," Janna said.

Mr. Vriend met her eyes. "I am glad to hear you say that. We came because we thought there would be so much more opportunity for you and Piet. I thought in a place like this you could become... well, whoever you wanted to be." He shook his head. "But perhaps I was wrong. I know your mother will never be completely happy here. This place will never be home for her."

"Let me get you something to eat," Janna said.

Mr. Vriend didn't seem to have heard her. "It was I who made the decision, and now I must live with the consequences. I can only pray that my choice was the right one for all of you. If only I could get a job..." He sank his head in his hands again.

"Everything will work out," Janna said awkwardly. "You'll feel better when Moeke comes back from Neerlandia."

But Mrs. Vriend did not come back until after the threshing had been done, and when she did she brought Piet,

Jakob and Willie so the house which had been lonely and quiet was suddenly full of boys and noise. Sara stayed behind to take care of her father, who had managed to join a road crew to pay off some of the taxes owing on the farm. But still Mr. Vriend did not get a permanent job, only some temporary ones which lasted a few days, a week at most. As a result, Janna didn't go back to school in the fall and when she got her money from Mrs. Randolph she handed it straight to Mrs. Vriend.

What made things worse was the fact that since Charles was back at school she saw him less often, and when he came into the kitchen with Norm or Geoff or Philip, she felt gawky and ugly in the shapeless apron she wore over her dress and tried to avoid them. Still, when Charles could walk with her in the evening under trees turned amber and gold, she forgot for the time that she was far from home and that the winter stretched out like an icy black tunnel in front of her. And as the evenings darkened and grew colder, and leaves spiralled from the trees above them like shoals of fishes glinting in the dying light of day, she and Charles walked closer together and the leaves crackled under their feet, and their laughter was as warm as it had been in the bright summer sun.

It was already October when Janna overheard Mrs. Randolph talking to Charles about her. She had left the house, but came back to fetch her money which she had left on top of the small refrigerator. Mrs. Randolph's voice in the passage overshadowed the faint click of Janna's opening the kitchen door.

"Where are you going, Charles?"

"Nowhere special," Charles replied.

"You're sneaking off to meet that girl, aren't you?" Mrs. Randolph demanded.

Janna froze. She dared not move in case the creaking of the floor announced her presence.

"What girl?"

"You know exactly whom I'm talking about," Mrs. Randolph said. "Janna. Our maid."

Charles didn't reply.

"Mrs. Fitzgerald has told me she has seen you two together almost every evening."

There was a pause. "So what?" Charles said eventually. "What's wrong with that?"

Janna took a step towards the fridge as Mrs. Randolph snorted in reply. "I shouldn't have to tell you, Charles. She is not your sort. You must choose more suitable companions. It's bad enough that you run around with someone like Norm, but Janna! Well!"

"What's wrong with Janna? I like her."

"And I like her too," Mrs. Randolph said coldly. "She is a nice girl. However, she comes from a different background, and she has not had your advantages. You would do far better to find your friends from amongst your own kind."

"Janna is my own kind. We have a lot in common."

Janna's blood was pounding as she grabbed her money. If she heard anymore, she would lose her self control.

"There are qualities you should look for in a companion," Mrs. Randolph went on, "qualities you won't find amongst the working classes, like refinement."

Janna reached the door and threw it open. Outside she leaned against the wall, taking great gulps of chilly air to cool her fury.

A moment later the door opened behind her. It was Charles. "Janna, I didn't know you were here."

"No. And I imagine your grandma didn't either."

"You heard." Charles buttoned up the jacket he was wearing. "I'm really sorry about that. But don't let it bother you. I've told you before that my father says she likes to pretend to be someone important because inside she feels that she's not. Don't take her seriously."

"But you?" Janna asked. "Do you take her seriously?"

Charles glanced behind him at the closed door. "I'm here, aren't I? Let's go." He patted a bulge in his jacket. "I've brought some paper and I'm going to make Willie a kite. It'll fly well in this wind."

The wind was cold. Janna shivered as he spoke and pulled her coat more tightly around her. It was too small to do up all the buttons, but there wasn't the money for a new one. "There's plenty of wear left in that one, Janna," Mrs. Vriend had said. "We can let it out." But even after it was let out, Janna shivered in the dark mornings as she walked to

Charles' house, along sidewalks buried in brittle brown leaves, past tree trunks stark against pale autumn skies. Sometimes it seemed that time had stopped and that Janna was entombed. At those times she struggled even to remember what her family looked like. It was as though she stared at their faces in mirrors which kept changing and distorting.

Despite the cold, Janna was relieved when the first snowfall arrived in November. It meant that spring was nearer, and when spring came, so would the painting. She stared out the window as she dusted the silver in the big display cabinet in the Randolphs' drawing room, watching the tiny flakes, dancing like dandelion fluff in the wind, grow larger and wetter, like splashes of soapy foam. By the time Janna had finished working, the neighbourhood was covered with a thick cloud of white.

"Isn't it swell?" Charles said when he walked home with her and they reached the hill which was packed with shrieking, laughing figures flying down the slope on bobsleds. "This is a smashing hill. I love sledding. Have you got a sled?"

Janna cupped her hands round her mouth and blew on her icy fingers. She stamped her frozen feet. "I don't think so."

"Never mind. We don't need one." He pointed at two boys toiling up the hill. "Look! There's Piet and Jakob. They've got a piece of cardboard. That'd be perfect. I wonder where they got it. And look at Willie. He's got something too. What is it?"

"It looks like Moeke's tea tray," Janna said. "I bet she won't be too happy about that. It's one she brought from Holland."

"Hey, Piet!" Charles lumbered through the snow towards him. "Let me get on that with you."

The following evening Charles brought his own sled with him. "I brought it for Willie," he explained as he carried it past the lighted shop windows on Jasper Avenue. "He says he's never been on a real sled."

Janna stopped to pull the large overshoes Mr. Vriend had given her back over her shoes. "He'll be scared if you go too fast."

"How about you?" Charles said.

"Of course I'm not scared," Janna said. "You should know that by now."

Even so, her stomach did lurch as the sled perched precariously on the edge of the precipice. "I didn't realize this hill was so steep."

"You are scared!" Charles exclaimed. "Move over. I'll go in front. You can sit behind me and I'll protect you."

Janna elbowed him out the way. "I don't need protecting," she retorted. "I'm going in front." She dived onto the sled.

"Wait!" Charles yelled. He landed with a thump behind her as the sled began to hurtle down the hill faster and faster until everything around them was blurred. Cold snow spurted in Janna's face and down her neck. Her overshoes fell off and her jacket flew open. And then with a whoosh the sled flew over a bump and into a snow bank. Janna was buried with Charles in a tangled heap in the snow.

Charles burst out laughing as he shook the snow out of his hair, his eyes and his mouth. "Some driver you are. Next time let me go in front and I'll get us to the bottom." He held out his hand to help Janna up.

Something happened as he took her hand. It was as though a current passed between them. For a moment they just stood looking at each other. In the soft light reflecting from the snow, Charles' eyes were deep, deep blue. Janna pulled her hand away and hid her eyes so that he wouldn't see her confusion.

"Hey, there's Willie!" Charles said. "Willie," he called. "Come and see. I brought you a sled."

Janna watched him leaping through the snow towards the little boy. She wanted to laugh and cry, although she wasn't sure why. All she could do was to roll the memory of Charles' hand holding hers around in her mind as she would savour chocolate in her mouth.

After that, there was something new between them which was enough to drive the smell of ammonia from Janna's nostrils and to make her think about spring with a mixture of anticipation and dread. It was only as Christmas approached that Janna's heart ached again, and the feeling that she did not belong, which she had pushed to the back of her mind, surfaced. She had to pretend to be excited when Piet, Jakob and Willie anticipated what Sinter Klaas would bring them on the fifth of December. And when Mrs. Vriend warned Willie that if he did not behave and do all his chores properly then Black Peter would carry him off in his sack, Janna wanted to take Willie on her lap and reassure him that there was no Black Peter and that Santa who ought to come on Christmas Eve, not on the fifth of December, never brought anyone coal. Only Charles' gift, a key-holder he had made in woodwork, cheered her up.

And when Christmas Eve came, Janna sat through church struggling against tears as she wondered what Roddy and her mother were doing. Later the Vriends sang carols around a Christmas tree decorated with real candles and tiny glass ornaments with shining strands of silver thread woven into them, and Janna noticed tears, shining like dewdrops in the candlelight, running down Mrs. Vriend's cheeks.

She smiled when she caught Janna's glance. "I'm not really sad," she said. "I'm very grateful for my children and my family."

Janna turned and stared at the flickering reflection of the candle flames in the frost-rimed window pane. She wished she could tell her mother that she loved her.

Chapter Thirteen

Christmas passed and Janna's heartache eased. As spring approached, there was much to take her mind off the long wait. In March, she and Charles took Willie to the ice carnival and they cheered Riverdale's hockey and broomball teams. They watched figure skating demonstrations and the recitations and presentations put on by schoolchildren. In April, tiny buds burst along the limbs of skeletal grey trees, and along the river the ice began to creak and groan and heave into peaks and pinnacles like great frozen waves. Each day the sounds of cracking ice grew louder and louder.

"Stay away from the river," Mr. Vriend warned them. "You know the ice is dangerous at this time of year." But they ignored him, and Janna, Piet, Willie and Jakob joined the growing crowds of people who hung over Dawson Bridge and strolled along the river bank speculating on the moment the ice would give and the river start to run.

"Everyone is betting," Charles said raising his voice over a thunderous crack as he and Janna leaned over the railing on the bridge. "Tomorrow I'm going to bring some money." He took Janna's hand briefly. "Maybe I'll win a fortune and you and I can run away together and get married and live happily ever after."

Janna blushed. Did he really mean that or was he joking? She wanted to ask him, but Charles was staring down at the peaks of ice. His expression had changed. "Sometimes," he said, "it feels as though one has no control over anything. Do you ever feel like that?"

"Often," Janna said. "Always." She stared at dead leaves blowing with the dust over the bridge. That was how she felt: tossed in the wind of her emotions, blown this way and that between longing and dread for Charles' cousin's arrival.

"One day," Charles said, "I'm going to make my own decisions and then I'll leave. I'm going to be a pilot and travel the world. You can come too if you want."

Janna's hands tightened round the bridge railing. If only that were a possibility. "I wish you could travel to my world," she whispered to herself. But she knew that even if he could, it would not help. One could not live in two worlds.

"By the way," Charles went on, "speaking of travel, we just got a letter from my father's cousin to say he's coming to Edmonton and bringing that painting you like."

"When?" Janna asked.

"The first of May," Charles said.

"That's the May festival," Janna said. It was only two

weeks away. In two weeks she would see her family again; it had been almost two years since she last saw them. She wondered how much they had changed. But could she leave Charles? She forced herself to control the tumult of mixed emotion flooding through her. "Willie's class is going to perform the Maypole dance. He's so cross that only the girls are allowed to do it."

Charles laughed. "He's right. The boys would do a far better job."

Janna made an effort to sound cheerful. "I'll tell Willie's teacher that you've volunteered."

"No, no. Tell her if she needs anyone to choose the May Queen, I'm available."

Janna rolled her eyes. "Who would you choose?"

"I'd choose you, of course." He blushed as he spoke.

"You would?" Janna felt suddenly light-headed. "I'd choose you too."

"Thanks," Charles said. "I've always wanted to be May Queen."

Janna lay in bed the night before the May festival tossing and turning and listening to the sounds of the night: the creaking of the house, a breeze nosing at the taped window, the distant hoot of a train whistle. It seemed that she had only just dozed off when Willie tugged at her sleeve in the morning. "It's the picnic today, Janna!" he squealed excitedly. "Tante says you must get up and help with breakfast while she makes our picnic lunch."

The day had come! Janna threw her arms around Willie and pulled him into bed with her. "I love you, you know," she whispered in his ear as he struggled to get free. But Willie was too excited to keep still. He bounced out of bed, and as Janna dressed she could hear his footsteps running through the house. "I'm going to enter the sack race and the obstacle race and the egg toss and the tug o' war and . . ."

"All right," Mrs. Vriend muttered good-naturedly. "We'll be ready soon."

Janna didn't participate in the events of the picnic. She watched torn between tears and laughter. Charles touched her arm. "Why weren't you in the three-legged race?"

Janna spun around. "I didn't see you come," she said. "How long have you been here?"

"I just arrived. I had to get out of the house. I've had a row with my grandma."

"What about?" Janna squeezed through the throng of spectators after him.

"She wanted me to go east to go to school in September," Charles said, taking her hand as they crossed the field towards the river. "I told her I wouldn't go."

"I bet she was mad."

"More than mad. She's threatening to make me leave school if I don't do what she wants." He flopped down under a tree. "I don't care. I'll work if I have to."

Janna lowered herself beside him. "But you should finish school," she said. "Education is important."

"I know. I'll take night school or something, but she can't make me leave you. I love you, Janna." He bent his head and touched her cheek with his lips.

Janna wanted to laugh and cry. She rested her head on his chest and longed to tell him the truth about herself. "Do you remember what I told you a long time ago? How I was staring at your grandma's painting, only it was on my grandma's wall, and I suddenly changed from the future and ended up with you?"

"By the way, we have the painting back," Charles said. "But don't joke now, Janna." Awkwardly his lips brushed hers, and then he kissed her. Janna clung to him. There was no point in trying to talk. No one would ever believe the truth.

She clung also to Mrs. Vriend before she left for work the next morning. "Are you feeling all right?" Mrs. Vriend asked her.

Janna nodded fighting tears. "Fine. I've just got something in my eye." She hugged Willie and then ruffled the spike on Piet's hair.

"Hey!" He swatted her hand away. Janna didn't retaliate. She wanted to hug him too, but he'd never understand. "Have a nice life," she said as she walked to the door.

And then she was at the Randolphs and outside the library door, her heart thumping against her ribs and when she opened the door, the painting was hanging just where it had hung before, above the fireplace. And as Janna raised her eyes and stared at the bush, the lady came gliding out. Janna felt a rush of panic — it was happening. It was really happening. What she had dreamed about for months was finally taking place. She felt as though she were falling. Faintly she heard air rushing past her ears, and the sound of weeping, and a crackling like flames, and then she lost consciousness.

Chapter Fourteen

Janna's eyelids fluttered awake. The smell of lavender water filled her nostrils and there was softness under her. She stirred, struggling to make sense of the blurred images in her mind. Where was she? And then she remembered. She jerked up in bed and looked around.

Through the window, the sky was tinged pearly pink. In the soft light Janna could make out the dresser covered with Omie's ornaments and the rosebud wallpaper. A light in the kitchen caught her eye. Janna slid off the high bed and peered round the bedroom door. Omie was sitting at the kitchen table sipping a cup of coffee, her hair a fuzzy white halo around her head. Janna's voice choked in her throat. "Omie," she whispered.

Omie looked up. "Hello, little love. Couldn't you sleep either? Do you want to join me for coffee?" She didn't sound at all surprised to see Janna or seem to notice anything different about her.

Janna didn't care. She gave Omie a hug. "I'll get it," she said.

"No, no. Let me." Omie walked over to the kettle. "Do you want coffee or would you prefer hot chocolate?"

"Uh... hot chocolate would be nice." Janna sank into a chair and stared at the shiny white appliances, clean white floor, and bright canisters along the countertop — all so modern — so familiar — so strange.

Omie placed the mug of hot chocolate on the table in front of her. "I hope you've had enough sleep. I had a terrible night. I had such strange dreams. I feel quite exhausted."

Janna took a sip of her drink. It was sweet, syrupy, wonderful. "Where's Mom?"

"Still asleep, I expect."

"She's here?" Janna jumped to her feet.

"Of course she's here..."

The rest of her sentence was lost as the door flew open and crashed against the doorstop. "Janna!" Roddy flew across the room and launched himself at her lap. His face was soft against her cheek and Janna held him tightly. He was as warm, soft and wriggly as she remembered.

Roddy squirmed free. "Can we go to the waterpark again today?"

"Yesterday was enough for me," Omie said. "Maybe today we can go to the zoo."

Janna's thoughts whirled. "We went to the waterpark yesterday?"

"The zoo!" Roddy slid off Janna's lap and scrambled onto Omie's. "Is it like Toronto zoo? We went to Toronto zoo, didn't we, Janna?"

Janna nodded and stared at Roddy. He didn't look any older than he had when she had last seen him. She picked up her cup and walked to the mirror in the hallway and gazed at her own reflection. It was like looking into the face of a stranger. She looked thirteen again: her hair was short and her figure flatter. She inspected her hands. They were smooth and pink. Dizzy and confused, Janna gulped her drink and made for the front door. She needed to think. A movement at the other end of the porch caught her attention as she stepped outside. She looked over to see the old man, Gramps, sitting in the shadows lighting a pipe. He waved the pipe in her direction. "Good morning." The warm smell of pipe smoke filled Janna's nostrils. It reminded her of Neerlandia.

The old man waved his pipe. "I'm going home soon, but I'll see you again tomorrow. My daughter has invited you all to tea."

Janna wasn't paying attention. She was staring at the street in front of Omie's house. So much looked the same as it had when she had last seen it — in 1935. The road was still lined with elms, gilded now in soft dawn light, taller and more straggly. The lilac hedge was still there, and some of the houses were the same. But much was different too: the blocks of apartments, the streetlights, the drone of city traffic.

"I'm looking forward to meeting your mother and grandmother," Gramps said.

Janna did not want to get into conversation. "I have to go and see if my mother's awake," was all she replied.

Vivian was sitting up in bed with a mug of coffee when Janna got to her room. "Hello," she said. "You're up early." Her smile was guarded.

Janna wanted to say that she wasn't up early at all. In 1935 she had had to get up considerably earlier to walk to Mrs. Randolph's. And in Neerlandia... Janna felt the spinning sensation start in her head again. She perched on the edge of the bed. "I came to say..." her voice trailed away. She couldn't tell her mother that she was glad to be back. "I came to say I'm sorry about... about last night." It wasn't hard to apologize. It had happened so long ago that it didn't matter anymore. Janna had discovered it was possible to learn to love someone. She loved all the Vriends, even Mr. Vriend once she had come to understand him. She would learn to love Dennis.

Vivian put down her cup and put her arms round Janna. "I appreciate your saying that, sweetheart. I'm sorry too. I should have been more sensitive. You don't have to come to the wedding if you don't want to. Of course I'd like you to be there, but it's your decision." She smiled at Janna and then cocked her head, scrutinizing her. "There's something different about you. What is it?"

Everything, Janna wanted to say. Everything is different. But she shook her head. "Nothing." She didn't want to think about the wedding yet. She wanted time to adjust to being home first. But it was something she had to deal with. "Do you love him?" She thought of the warm feeling she carried inside her for Charles and it hurt.

"Dennis? Of course I love him. I wouldn't be marrying him otherwise."

"And did you love Dad?"

"Janna, you must believe me. I loved your father and nothing will change that. In my heart I will always love him. But he's gone, and now I love Dennis too."

Janna thought she could never love anyone else besides Charles. "I don't see how that's possible."

Vivian put her arm around Janna's shoulder. "It's because I've experienced love that I'm able to love again. It'll be different this time, but it will still be love. Love takes many forms. I hope you will find that out."

Janna hoped her mother was right. "I'll come to the wedding," she said.

"That's wonderful." Vivian took Janna's hands. "Let's leave everyone else and go out for the day. Perhaps we could go shopping. I'd love it if you would help me choose something to wear for the wedding. And you'll need something too. What do you say?"

It was already evening when Janna and her mother returned from the malls. Vivian dumped a pile of parcels on the kitchen table. "How was the zoo? We had a wonderful day. Just wait until you see what we bought." She pulled a box out of one of the packets and opened the lid. "Look. Janna's dress for the wedding. Isn't it beautiful?"

Omie glanced at Janna out of the corner of her eyes. "Lovely," she agreed.

"I decided I would go to the wedding after all," Janna explained with a smile. "Mom promised the food would be good."

Roddy interrupted before Omie could respond. "Look what I found, he said bouncing into the kitchen, brandishing two glass elephants, one in each hand. "Elephants, like at the zoo."

"Roddy! Give them to me." Omie cried, springing towards him.

Janna took advantage of the ensuing tussle to escape from the room. She needed to be alone. It had been a good day with her mother, but it had been odd to eat lunch in a restaurant and to spend money as though it were nothing out of the ordinary when just the day before every cent had been precious. She felt the same curious sense of being different from everyone else that she had felt in the past. Perhaps the feeling wasn't altogether a bad thing. Perhaps she was different from everyone else. Wasn't that what her father had always told her?

Janna walked onto the porch and leaned on the railings. So many things had reminded her of Charles. The old movie theatre she and Charles had walked by every evening was still there, restored now to look exactly as it had then. The bridge over the river was the same, although no streetcars creaked precariously over the top level. Omie's house, even the haunting melody on the piano she could hear now from the house next door, made her think of Charles.

She didn't know how she could bear never seeing him again, never knowing what happened to him, whether he had been part of the war that lay ahead of him, whether he had lived happily ever after. And she wished desperately that she had tried harder to tell him the truth about who she was and where she came from. It was as though a lie lay between them.

Later that night, as she lay in bed, Janna looked at the picture on the wall through half closed eyes and wondered, as she had many times before, why the lady had taken her back to the past. She hadn't accomplished anything while she was there. All that had happened was that she had to live now with heartache and the sense that the story wasn't finished, that something wasn't resolved. And she would never know what. Unless she went back again. One more time.

A breeze ruffled the partly closed drapes at the window, and pale moonlight rippled across the room. The corner of the curtain lifted on a puff of air and the moon cast a pale ray across the lake water. Janna thought she could see the waves rippling, and faintly, faintly she heard a voice calling.

She got out of bed and padded across the floor to the window. She threw open the curtains and silver light flooded the room. Janna turned to look at the painting. The lady was waiting for her.

Chapter Fifteen

Janna landed with a thump that took her breath away. She opened her eyes and scrambled to her feet. She was not in the library, where she had expected to be. She was standing outside Charles' back door on a cold grey day, shivering. Thin snow crusted on the ground and scabbed the naked limbs of the trees. Janna pulled her sweater closer and glanced at a pile of boxes, an old lamp, a broken chair, and a worn mat stacked by the steps.

The back door opened suddenly and Mrs. Randolph came out clutching a bundle of old newspapers. She looked older than Janna remembered, bent, shrivelled, broken almost.

She stiffened when she saw Janna. "What do you want?"

Janna shrank before the venom in her voice. "Charles," she stammered.

"I don't know how you have the gall to come here," Mrs. Randolph spat out, straightening her bent back. "You must know he's missing."

"Missing?" Janna repeated stupidly. Missing. Missing!

Missing? The word repeated in her head. What did Mrs. Randolph mean?

Mrs. Randolph's eyes narrowed spitefully. "He would never have married you anyway. You do know that, don't you? His last letters were full of Angela Holbottom. They were going to get engaged." She glowered triumphantly at Janna. "He would have married Angela. Angela was very suitable." And then she seemed to fold like a deflating balloon. She dropped the newspapers and stumbled back into the kitchen. The door swung shut behind her.

Janna stood in the bleak backyard staring at the closed door. Charles was gone — missing and he had loved someone else. A gust of icy wind swept a crumpled page of the newspaper across Janna's ankles. She bent down to free it.

The door opened as she straightened up. "Can I help you, love?" a stout woman wearing an apron asked.

Janna was staring at the faded newspaper in her hand. The date on it was November 1940. "Is this . . . I mean when . . . Can you tell me what happened to Charles?"

The woman clucked sympathetically. "Nobody knows." She glanced behind her and closed the door. "It's a terrible shame. The missus got a telegram about how he was shot down in France. Missing in action, it said."

"He was a pilot," the woman went on. "Nearly went out of her mind, Mrs. Randolph did. His father too." The woman indicated the piles of junk lying around them. "His father went back east and now she's moving as well, throwing all this out. She's going to her sister."

"Perhaps Charles is all right," Janna said, shaking from cold within and without. "Perhaps they'll find him."

The stout woman shrugged. "Not much hope for them pilots, I heard." She glanced behind her as a shrill voice sounded from inside the house. "She's right cranky this morning." The woman leaned so close Janna could smell onions on her breath. "I heard from the lady who worked here before that Mrs. Randolph threatened to cut him off without a penny because of some girl, so he up and joined the air force. Don't know what happened to the girl though. Haven't seen her around here since I been here."

"Was it the girl he was getting engaged to?" Janna whispered.

The shrill voice inside the house called again.

The woman hurried up the stairs. "Not so's I would know," she said. She paused for a moment. "Someone called Jane? Janet? Something like that." She shook her head. "I don't remember. But I can't chat anymore, dearie. I'll be in trouble already." She closed the door behind her.

Janna leaned against the wall of the house trying to suck warmth from its surface. The wind blew again: the newspaper swirled across the yard; an old tin can rattled from the heap of junk across the icy snow; an empty box blew off the stack. And then Janna saw it: a frame, face down on the pile of discarded boxes. She flew to it, grabbed it, turned it over. It was Omie's painting. Hugging it against her chest, she scurried behind the skeletal lilac hedge. At least she had something of Charles. But as she turned the painting over to look at it, strong hands gripped her wrists. It was the lady from the painting, pale and white.

"No!" Janna struggled to get free. "Not yet! I have to find out what happened to Charles." But she was already spinning, tumbling dizzily through cold darkness.

Janna felt sick when she woke up the next morning. Her room wavered in front of her eyes and her stomach lurched when she moved. She lay still, remembering — remembering that Charles had wanted to marry her. Longing, like thirst, seeped through her. And then she remembered where she was and that Charles was lost. "No!" Janna's voice broke from her throat and echoed round her walls. Her eyes sought the painting. This time there was no question about whether she should risk returning to the past. She couldn't always carry this ache around with her. She had to know what had happened.

Her eyes met bare wall. Janna jerked up, fighting nausea. The painting had fallen off the wall and was lying on the floor. One corner of the frame was shattered. She staggered out of bed and propped it against the wall in a patch of sunlight. But even in the bright rush of morning light, the painting remained dull and lifeless. The pale brush strokes behind the bush were barely discernible. Janna tugged at her curtains to let in more light, but nothing happened. It was as though the light from within the painting had gone.

She angled the frame in several directions. Still nothing happened. Why wasn't it working?

"Are you awake?" Omie asked, peeking her head round Janna's door. "Come into the kitchen and have tea with me. Your mother and Roddy have gone for a walk so I could do with some company. I've been looking through old photographs. You might be interested in seeing them."

Omie pointed at a tattered brown album lying on the kitchen table as Janna slumped into a chair. Janna opened the page listlessly. The photographs were faded, old-fashioned and sometimes blurred: a group of children, a group of adults and children, two children with some chickens, five children in front of a log house. The house caught Janna's attention. It was familiar.

She stared more closely at the four children. There were two girls and three boys. Janna focussed on the girls. The taller one had blonde pigtails and a wide smile. Janna squinted at the page, held it up to the light. "It's Sara," she breathed. "And that's Piet, and Willie, and Jakob."

"What did you say, dear?" Omie passed Janna a cup of tea.

"Who are these people?" Janna asked.

Omie fished in her pocket for her glasses, and then pulled the photograph album closer. She peered at the photograph. "This one is my brother, Piet." She jabbed her finger at a blurred face. "Just look at his hair. It never would lie flat. And these other two are my cousins, Jakob and Willie. And that's my cousin Sara."

Janna felt dazed. Nothing made any sense. "And who's that?" she asked pointing at the girl beside Sara, a thin dark haired girl with a solemn determined face and dark eye-brows, a girl whose face Janna had seen in the mirror every morning for a long time.

"Why that's me," Omie said. "That was taken when we were staying with my uncle Klaas at Neerlandia."

Janna's skin prickled with goose-bumps. "But you're not Dutch."

Omie laughed. "Of course I am. Well, I'm Canadian, I suppose, but I was born in Holland."

"But you don't speak Dutch."

"Not much anymore. My father encouraged us to speak English. He said we had to assimilate if we wanted to be at home. And then Opie wasn't Dutch. But I wanted you to call me Oma, until you started calling me Omie when you were a baby." Omie studied the photograph again and shook her head. "How quickly a lifetime passes."

"Where are they — your brother and your cousins?" Janna asked.

Omie's face clouded. "My brother Piet was killed in the Second World War, and my cousins left Canada and went to the United States after my uncle lost his farm. I didn't see them all that often after that, but we did keep in touch. Sara married a Hollander and went back to Holland. Jakob died a few years ago, but I still get a Christmas card from Willie." Omie smiled. "I was always very fond of Willie. He's living in a retirement home now."

Janna gaped at her for a moment. Willie was an old man. And so would Charles be if he were alive. Janna turned back to the album and started flipping the pages, looking for him. She found him in the background of what looked like a picnic. "Who's that?" she asked, trying to keep the urgency from her voice.

Omie stared at the picture without answering. "That's a boy I used to know," she said finally. "His name was Charles. As a matter of fact, he used to live in this very house."

Janna's fingers tightened round the cover of the album. "What happened to him?"

Omie got up and carried her cup to the sink. "I don't really know. He joined the air force without telling me. He knew I didn't think it was a good idea. I wrote to him but I never found out if he received my letters because I never heard from him. My parents moved, you see, so he didn't have my address. And later I heard that he was missing." Omie's voice was so quiet that Janna had to strain to hear her.

"And then?" she demanded.

Omie shrugged. "I can't tell you. His family went away. I moved. I met your grandfather." She ran the water into the sink. "But you know, even after all these years, I'd still like to find out what happened to him. I was thinking about that just yesterday and I thought I might see if there were any war records that I could consult — just to satisfy curiosity. Silly really."

Janna's mind was skidding like a car out of control. Why had the painting dropped her into Omie's life? "Did you love Charles, Omie?" she asked.

Omie turned from the sink. "Oh yes," she said softly. "I did then. He was my first love. You never forget your first love."

Janna felt as though she were struggling through gauze as she walked back to her room. Charles was her first love too. How was it possible that they both loved Charles? Had he loved both of them? In her room, the painting was lying on the floor. As Janna lifted it, a damaged piece of frame fell off. She bent and retrieved the fragment and tried to wedge it back onto the painting, but something was in the way. Janna turned the piece of frame over and examined it.

She saw the problem immediately. The frame appeared to be splitting. She looked again. No, it wasn't splitting. There was something stuck to the wood. Gently Janna levered at it. It was paper, folded into a narrow strip and wedged into a crack.

With a pounding heart, Janna unfolded it. The paper was brittle and cracked along the folds, but the writing inside was quite legible.

My dearest Janna,

I wish I could hold you and say good-bye one last time, but tomorrow I leave for my squadron. I know you are unhappy about this, but let me tell you again that this is something I have to do if we two are ever to have any kind of life together. I know there are risks, and that is why I have left this message to tell you that I will always love you. If anything happens, don't forget that. Nothing will ever change that for me.

Yours for eternity,
Charles

Janna clutched the letter. At least she could be sure now that Mrs. Randolph had been lying to her: Charles had never loved anyone else. And then Janna cried. She cried for Charles who had gone away to war and had not come back. And she cried for herself because she would never see him again. Her pillow was wet with her tears and her eyes were red and sore before she thought of Omie and realized that the letter must be for Omie too. It was Omie with whom she had changed places and Omie whom Charles must have known and loved in all those missing years.

Janna splashed her face with cold water at the kitchen sink and brushed her hair. She tapped at Omie's door. "What is it?" Omie called.

"It's me, Janna." She pushed open the door. "Sorry to disturb you."

Omie was sitting in an upright chair by the window. "Come in," she said. "I was just about to lie down. Be a dear and tell your mother that I'm not feeling up to a visit with the neighbours this afternoon. I've had so many bad nights lately."

"I don't want to go either," Janna said. "But I wanted to tell you that the painting fell off the wall — your special painting, I mean. The picture's fine, but the frame broke and I . . ." She hesitated for a moment. To give away the letter was like parting with her heart. "I found this." She passed the paper to Omie.

Omie began to read. Her lips quivered and then she broke into a smile that transformed her face. "This letter is from Charles, the boy we were speaking about. Did you read it? Oh little love, even after all this time it makes me happy to hear that he did love me."

He loved me too, Janna's heart cried silently. "The letter is written to Janna. That's my name, not yours."

"Janna is my second name," Omie said as she reread the letter. "When I was a child, I liked it better and everybody called me by that name. Didn't you know you were named after me?"

Perhaps she had known. In her confusion, Janna wasn't sure. She wasn't sure of anything.

Omie was smiling again. "Charles' mother told me he was going to marry some other girl. At first I didn't believe her, but when I didn't hear anything from him, I couldn't help wondering. I can't believe that this has been in that picture all the while. That picture belonged to his family, you know. His grandmother threw it out when she moved and I took it so that I would have something of his."

Perhaps, Janna thought, that was why she had gone into Omie's past — so that she could find the message for her now. But that didn't seem enough reason. Omie might be happier, but Janna felt as though she had shards of glass piercing her soul and there was still so much she didn't understand. "Did you love Opie when you got married?"

Omie pulled a tissue out of the box on her bedside table. "Of course I did, little love. We had forty good years together and I wouldn't exchange them for anything. But a little part of me has always loved Charles and I suppose always will." She grinned. "He was a very good-looking boy, Charles." She smiled and laid the cracked paper carefully inside a large black Bible beside her bed. "Well, I don't think I will lie down after all. And maybe I can manage to face our tea engagement. You'll come too, won't you Janna? Just for moral support."

Chapter Sixteen

Judy Mason greeted them when Vivian knocked at the neighbour's door later that afternoon. "I'm so pleased you could make it. My father has been so looking forward to meeting you all."

Omie who was hiding behind Janna muttered something under her breath.

"I'm pleased to meet you," Vivian said, stepping forward and extending her hand to the old man standing behind his daughter.

"Dad," Mrs. Mason said. "This is my next-door neighbour, Mrs. Meyers. I think you've already met her granddaughter, Janna."

Omie was staring at Gramps. "Have we met before?" she asked. "You look familiar."

"This is my father," Mrs. Mason went on, "Charles Randolph."

Janna felt as though she were going to faint. "Charles?" she whispered. Electric shocks spiked down her arms.

"Charles?" Omie said in a cracked voice, grabbing onto Janna's arm for support. "Is it possible?"

Gramps started. He stared at Omie as though he had seen a ghost. Janna had never noticed before what very blue eyes he had.

"Janna Vriend?" Gramps said taking a step forward.

"You two know each other?" Mrs. Mason asked, looking from one to the other. "What a coincidence."

Janna sank into a chair. Gramps was *Charles*. So that was it. She had had to go into Omie's life to get them back together. She scrutinized him, trying to see the young man she knew. For a second she did see him, the Charles he had been, a laughing boy with very blue eyes and a wide smile. But then the image flickered, wavered, dissolved and she was looking at an old man with a kindly weathered face, twinkling eyes, and a warm smile. And as she saw him, this new Charles, some of the splinters in Janna's heart melted.

"I can't believe it," Gramps said. "I just can't believe it." He looked from Janna to Omie. "I knew there was something very special about you the moment I met you," he told Janna. "Now I know what it is." Then he took Omie's hand and it was as though everyone else in the room ceased to exist. "Where did you go? I came back and you weren't there."

Omie was holding tightly onto Gramps' hand and staring at him. "I was told you were missing. I thought you'd died."

Gramps stroked Omie's hand. "I spent some time in France, but I did write as soon as I could."

Vivian and Mrs. Mason both looked stunned. Mrs. Mason beckoned. "Come into the kitchen. It sounds as though they have a lot to catch up on."

There was a boy standing by the sink, someone Janna had never seen before. "Hi," he said, extending his hand. "I'm Chuck." He had a wide smile, a mop of dark curly hair and eyes as blue as a mountain lake. "My mom says you're new here and you don't know anyone. Do you want to go biking? There are great cycle paths in the ravine."

Janna's heart was soaring. "I'd love to," she said. "You don't by any chance have a skull collection in the ravine, do you?"

Chuck ran his hand through his hair and his eyes widened in surprise. "How did you know that? Of course, I don't collect skulls anymore, but I used to and they probably are still there. Shall we go and look?"

Somewhere in the distance Janna thought she could hear music. She smiled. "Let's go."

ABOUT THE AUTHOR

Lynne Fairbridge was born in South Africa and moved to Rhodesia, now Zimbabwe, at the age of eight. She graduated from universities in both countries and then taught high school English and history until she immigrated to Canada in 1977. For the past few years, she taught at Concordia University College. In 1986 she began writing for young adults, and her first book, *My Sister Did It,* was published in 1989. Her second book, *In Such a Place,* won the sixth Alberta Writing for Youth Competition. Until her recent untimely death, she lived with her husband and children on an acreage in Sherwood Park, Alberta, where she wrote her fifth novel, *Tangled in Time.*